A ROYAL PAIN . . .

When the queen mentioned how delighted she was to have Felippa visit her with the obviously adored little Juan, I thought it was time to bring up the topic I had been dying to touch upon.

"Why do you suppose those men were trying to kidnap Juan?"

My God. The last time I saw looks of such intense shock was when one of my breasts popped out of my décolletage at the Duke of Westminster's dinner table when I bent down to pick up an earring.

NOBLESSE OBLIGE

Cynthia Smith

BERKLEY PRIME CRIME, NEW YORK

**To William Forest Pannier,
with all my love.**

NOBLESSE OBLIGE

A Berkley Prime Crime Book / published by arrangement with
the author

PRINTING HISTORY
Berkley Prime Crime edition / November 1996

The Putnam Berkley World Wide Web site address is
http://www.berkley.com

ISBN: 0-425-15549-8

Berkley Prime Crime Books are published
by The Berkley Publishing Group,
200 Madison Avenue, New York, NY 10016.
The name BERKLEY PRIME CRIME and the BERKLEY PRIME CRIME
design are trademarks belonging to Berkley Publishing Corporation.

PRINTED IN THE UNITED STATES OF AMERICA

10 9 8 7 6 5 4 3 2 1

Acknowledgments

This is usually where the author reels off a list of friends and relatives who kindly read her manuscript and whose wonderful suggestions made it into the finished product.

I showed this manuscript to and followed the advice of only my excellent agent, Judith Riven and fine editor, Natalee Rosenstein, both professionals whose opinions I highly respect. I wouldn't think of showing it to anyone else—what the hell do they know?

In my very first book (this is my eighth) I thanked my typist whose patience in deciphering my annotations I appreciated. In that vein, let me give my deepest thanks to the inventor of my marvelous Compaq Presario.

I guess what I'm trying to say here is that if you find any fault with this book, and I fervently hope you don't, it's basically mea culpa.

Cynthia Smith
Rye, NY

I

I WAS ANNOYED. Why is that car on a pedestrian walkway with its motor running? The Parc de Bruxelles is one of my favorite sylvan refuges from the clatter of trams and tour buses in Brussels. So why is that man sitting in his car, spoiling my tranquility and polluting the crisp spring air with odoriferous exhaust from his running motor?

This lovely park is situated in front of the royal palace where the black, yellow, and red Belgian flag was flying to announce that the king and queen were currently in residence. I had walked into the park to rest up from my visit to Le Musée d'Art Ancien. As a rule, I never step foot in a museum when I am in foreign ports since I see no reason to spend hours with paintings that at some point will undoubtedly be on special loan to the Metropolitan Museum of Art in New York City, one of my three hometowns. I much prefer spending my time with those elements of the national soul that cannot travel, like neighborhoods and the people. But I can't pass up the chance to enjoy the works of Pieter Brueghel, the great Flemish six-teenth-century "peasant painter" who was the first to portray ordinary people and everyday life in-stead of religious themes and stuffy aristocrats. I love his lusty village scenes and get a real kick out of finding a new significant detail in the corner of a favorite painting that I had missed before.

I had arrived in Brussels only yesterday to house-sit for some friends who had offered me their penthouse flat for two weeks while they re-turned home to America for the wedding of their son. Belgium is not one of the usual Grand Tour destinations. It has no "major attractions," like the Eiffel Tower or Buckingham Palace, for the unad-venturous tourist who needs a checklist of sights to be seen in order to impress the folks back home; its history is unfamiliar; and its royals are nice nor-mal folk whose antics never appear in the tabloids. All of which makes it one of my favorite spots be-cause it offers the thrill of discovering your own special finds, like turning a corner and suddenly coming upon a soaring belfry tower dating back to the 1200's, or a stunning medieval square filled with colorful streaming pennants and heraldic flags.

After spending two hours indoors, I needed to walk through this quiet place of trees and reflecting pools that, once a battleground, had been trans-formed into a French garden in 1835. I think it's one of the loveliest parks in Europe, besides being the setting of one of my favorite books, *The Profes-sor* by Charlotte Brontë.

I was deciding whether I should find a policeman and have him chase that car and driver off the walkway, or take my usual direct action and tell off the bastard myself. Suddenly I heard a commotion and saw a dark heavily mustached man racing toward the car clutching a small blond boy in his arms who was squirming and yelling, followed by a woman who was waving her arms and screaming and two uniformed men who were five yards behind her. The driver of the car revved his motor and leaned back to open his rear door, and I suddenly realized why he was waiting in that spot. Although most people today have a personal policy of strict noninvolvement, my instinct is to take part in other people's scenarios. So I bent down, picked up a rock, and hurled it at the driver's head where it connected with a satisfying *thwack!*, and he fell unconscious over the steering wheel with blood pouring down his shirt collar. His cohort, seeing the intended getaway aborted, dropped the child and started zigzagging his way out of the park. The woman and I reached the boy at the same time while the two uniformed men continued to run, and I heard yelling and gunshots. She picked up the crying boy and rocked him soothingly in her arms.

"Oh, mio querido. Mio pequeño querido!"

Then she turned to me, with tears streaming down her face.

"Dios Mio! Esta usted una ángel de cielos?" and she began a rapid outpouring that, although I do pretty well in Spanish, became almost incomprehensible. But the meaning was pretty clear; I was unquestionably a mixture of the Pope and El Cid and had been sent there by divine Providence. Her gratitude

was nice, but now that I knew the child was safe, I was more interested in knowing the outcome of the pursuit of the perpetrators. I didn't have to wait long. Within minutes, the park was swarming with police and an ambulance arrived to remove the man I had beaned and his friend, who had apparently been wounded in the shoulder. Having lived in New York and London where big city constabulary usually reach the crime scene well after all the blood has congealed, I was impressed with the stunning rapidity of Brussels' police response. Either they are incredibly efficient, or this almost-kidnapped child is from a family of great importance. The nanny did not speak in French or Flemish, the two native tongues of Belgium, which means they are visitors but obviously not your ordinary tourists.

"Pardon, madame. . . ." I looked up to see one of the policemen who had chased the would-be assailant, and I started to question him eagerly in French to find out what had happened.

"You are English? Or American?" said a soft voice, and I noticed a tall, Burberry-coated, sandy-haired man with startling deep blue eyes standing next to the gendarme. From the way the policeman stepped back, it was apparent this was a higher authority.

"Is my French that bad?" I asked.

He smiled—and I noticed the way it lit up his face. "No, actually it's quite good. It is just that your accent seems somewhat divided."

"So is my life." And I smiled right back. "But I am American."

His eyebrows went up—rather charmingly, I

thought—and he shrugged. This was not the moment for personal lifestyle revelation, but my snap decision was that he and I would get to that at a later date. I always find it prudent to divulge details only on a need-to-know-now basis. The fact that I split my year among my three residences in New York, London, and Vila do Mar, Portugal, was something that could come out over dinner and a glass of wine. You see, I had noticed that besides being extremely attractive, he wore no wedding ring.

"I am Inspector Albert Heist."

"That must be a rather difficult name for a policeman," I said.

"Perhaps in America," he said. "But here in Belgium it is the name of a town, not an activity."

"May I see your I.D., please?" I asked.

He held up an identification folder which, to his apparent surprise and slight amusement, I examined closely. In my work, skepticism is a basic tool and I am never impressed by a flashed I.D. no matter how official it looks. In some countries, sanitation inspectors display documents that bear more stamps and seals than the Vietnam peace treaty.

"*Commissaire de la Police Judiciaire*, like Inspector Maigret. Obviously this is more than an overtime-parking violation," I said. In Belgium, city mishaps are taken care of by the local police. National, international, and diplomatic matters are handled by an elite group called the Judicial Police, consisting of plainclothes inspectors and uniformed men who are known as Gendarmerie rather than police. I handed the folder back to him and asked, "Who is this Spanish child?"

"How did you know he was Spanish?" he asked quickly.

"The woman spoke Castilian," I answered.

He looked puzzled. "That is different than the Spanish spoken in other countries?"

"*Thi, thi*," I answered—rather wittily, I thought—but of course he didn't get it. "The *s* in pure Castilian is pronounced *th*," I said. "It's the form of Spanish spoken in Spain."

That tidbit of linguistic trivia came not because I have a huge store of arcane knowledge, which I do, but because I had a pronounced lisp as a child which made me persona gracias to my Spanish teachers, who kept commending me for my Castilian accent. Unfortunately, what is considered normal in Seville was regarded as unacceptable in Rye, New York, and I was subjected to years of tedious corrective speech classes until they successfully loosened my frenum so that I could have perfect impediment-free diction. (Don't bother running to the dictionary to look up "frenum": it's that small membrane under the tongue which, when too tight, is said to cause lisping.)

"You are very observant, Miss . . ."

"Rhodes. Emma Rhodes," I said with a smile.

He turned and said something rapidly in Flemish to the gendarme, who nodded and left.

"Miss Rhodes, that was rather quick thinking on your part. What made you realize an abduction was in progress?"

"The only other thing it might have been was a custody battle situation of divorced parents. But that very dark man didn't look like the father of that very blond boy, and the child didn't react like he was with Daddy—he was screaming his little head off. And the two police in hot pursuit made it apparent that something serious was happening."

"Taking action against the driver of the car was a very clever tactic," he said.

"What was my choice? I thought for a moment I might tackle the running man, but I'm much better at baseball than football, so I opted for my more effective area of expertise."

The inspector's beeper went off and he held it to his ear for a moment. Then he turned to me.

"Miss Rhodes, may I invite you to come with me to meet the child's family? They are most anxious to thank you in person."

I like appreciation, of course, but I'm uncomfortable with displays of emotion and I'd already had my fill with the nanny. Actually, the gratitude I'm used to usually comes in the form of a nice fat check. But this was strictly a pro bono episode. I didn't look forward to having my hand clutched by a pair of teary-eyed parents while listening to a paean of thanks. It's like being serenaded in a restaurant by a strolling violinist; one never knows quite where and how to look during his performance. Inspector Heist noticed my hesitation.

"Come, it is not far from here. And don't you want to know more details about this attempted crime that you so skillfully and courageously thwarted?"

Who says flattery will get you nowhere? But I was curious to find out what this was all about. And I am a sucker for perceptive articulate men.

II

WE DROVE THROUGH the park toward the royal palace and then, to my surprise, swung around through the gates into an interior courtyard. I noticed the uniformed guards recognized the inspector and waved us on. I was becoming more and more intrigued and tried to recall which dignitaries were visiting Brussels at the moment. We got out of the car and Inspector Heist led me up a small flight of stairs to a large set of double doors located on the side of the palace. The doors were opened by a liveried servant who had apparently been notified of our arrival by the gate guard. The servant led us to a small, elegant drawing room. Gilt chairs and sofas upholstered in green silk matched the gold-trimmed wall panels. A beautiful marquetry desk stood in the corner, and a series of small crystal-and-gilt chandeliers were suspended from a richly ornamented carved ceiling. Over the sofa was a Gobelin tapestry; portraits of presumed earlier Belgian royalty covered the other walls.

"Won't you please sit down?" said the inspector, motioning me to one of the pull-up chairs next to the sofa. "They should be here shortly."

Within minutes, the door at the far end of the room opened and two women entered. The older one was rather tall and slim with gray-streaked black hair. She was dressed in a very simple but expensively tailored plum-colored dress with an amethyst-and-gold pin on the shoulder. She seemed a mixture of shyness and confidence, and I liked her immediately. The younger woman wore a cherry-red Chanel suit. At first glance she seemed to be another of that cliché clique of so-called socialites of the bony blonde genre. But then you noticed a special elegance that made you realize she was the genuine article upon whom all the others tried to model themselves—but couldn't quite make it. As the older woman approached, Inspector Heist bowed.

"Your Majesty, this is Miss Emma Rhodes."

Good lord. Queen Fabiola!

I stood up quickly and probably for the first time in my life was awed and—if you can believe it—speechless. I'm not unaccustomed to royalty—some of my best friends are earls and baronesses, and I've spent many boring evenings with some of the many anachronistic members of dethroned European nobility who pass their lives waiting to be called back to rule over nations whose current populations know them only as names in history books. But Fabiola had been a full-fledged reigning monarch who by her actions had proven herself to be a true queen and was universally beloved by all Belgians. When her husband, King Baudouin, died at age sixty-two in 1993, his brother Albert assumed the throne, but I had heard that a small wing of the huge palace was given to Fabiola for lifetime use.

The queen stepped forward and held her hand out to me with a lovely smile.

"Miss Rhodes—my niece and I owe you a great debt. It was her son you saved." She turned to the blond woman. "This is my niece, Contessa Felippa de Rojas Sandoval."

Of course, the Spanish connection. Fabiola de Mora y Aragon was a colorless thirtyish woman from an aristocratic Spanish family when she astounded Europe by being chosen by the handsome blond Prince Baudouin to be his bride. The most eligible royal catch of the time, he was pursued by international beauties, heiresses, and every European royal family with a marriageable daughter. The eldest son of King Leopold III, who was forced to abdicate when his people turned against him for having surrendered to the Germans early on in World War II, the prince assumed the throne when he reached twenty-one in 1951. As he approached the age of thirty, which was considered old for an unmarried monarch, international nobility was becoming desperate. Every woman in the world was pursuing him—what on earth was he looking for? Imagine their shock when he announced his engagement in 1960, not to some royal beauty or glamorous nymphet or Grace Kelly-like movie star, but to an undistinguished Spanish woman of whom no one had ever heard, and who was—horror of horrors—older than he. Over the years, their union turned out to be probably the most successful royal marriage in Europe. Their love for each other was evident to all who knew them. And Queen Fabiola had proven herself to be a kind and caring woman who was devoted to her adopted country. Why did Baudouin choose this simple quiet woman to be his wife? He was probably wise enough to recognize that teenage royal bimbos may be nice to look at, but what do you talk about? And glamorous stars may be nice to visit, but hell to live with. Obviously she made him happy and comfortable and made his palace a home. What more could any king want? One wonders if Prince Charles doesn't wish he had made a similar choice.

"*Muchas gracias*, Miss Rhodes," said the contessa as she stepped forward to grasp my hand. "You have my everlasting gratitude." I looked directly at her and was surprised to see a strength and intelligence that is so rarely seen on aristocratic faces. She was stylish and elegant and I guessed in her early thirties. Her blond hair was worn pulled tightly back, a style that could only be worn with those finely chiseled cheekbones and nose. Small sapphire earrings matched the pin on her lapel as well as the deep blue of her eyes.

"Little Juan is very dear to me," said the queen. "You have done my family a great service, Miss Rhodes." Then she tilted her head and surveyed me for a moment, a small smile on her lips. "My men tell me you handled the matter with a rather unique and surprising efficiency."

"Unique, surely, but surprising, no, *querida tía*," said the contessa firmly. "It is only men who are surprised when a woman acts with speed, strength, and quick wit."

Aha, a feminist. I heard Inspector Heist clear his throat. "Perhaps it was the means rather than the gender that we found unexpected, Madame— much as the Philistines reacted to David."

"Touché, Inspector," said the queen as we all laughed. "But come, let us not just stand about. You must join us for tea, Miss Rhodes. Inspector?"

"No, thank you, Your Majesty. I'd better get back to headquarters to find out what interrogation has learned about these two men."

I noticed a quick look pass between the queen and her niece. Was that fear? But why?

"Miss Rhodes, I'll leave a man here to get you back to your apartment in Uccle." He smiled at the surprise on my face. "Did you think we would take you into the royal palace to meet our queen without first knowing all about you? We know that you are a writer who is staying at the flat of William and Diane Reed at Avenue Hamoir in Uccle." He smiled in smug satisfaction, obviously awaiting accolades for his supreme efficiency. Big deal.

"My compliments to your computer, Inspector."

My public identification has always been "writer" since I cannot think of any description of my unique profession that would be comprehensible to most people.

"What we don't know is where you learned to throw so swiftly and accurately, and did you fully realize your danger if that man was armed?"

"To answer your first question, Inspector—I was the star pitcher of the Camp High Point softball team for five years running. And that answers your second question, too. Sure I knew he could have a gun—but I also knew that he'd never be able to use it. Hey, I pitched six no-hit games one summer." I smiled. "At a distance of ten feet, I couldn't miss."

He bowed to the queen, headed toward the door, and turned to me. "Miss Rhodes, I'll be in touch with you later today. Er, to discuss some of the details of this matter—your impressions, and so on."

"Certainly, I'll be available," I said. Let him take that any way he chooses.

The queen and the contessa sat down on the sofa, and I took the chair facing them.

The rear door opened and a servant wheeled in a tea trolley.

"We call it 'tea,' but actually we mostly prefer coffee, Miss Rhodes," said the queen. "Which would you like?"

She poured my coffee—"Black, please."—and handed the cup to the servant who stood at her elbow. He placed it in front of me along with an empty cake plate and then proffered a silver tiered tray filled with a stunning assortment of tarts and cakes.

Many international gourmets claim that Brussels' patisseries as well as restaurants are superior to those of Paris. Since becoming headquarters for NATO and the European Community and thus in effect the capital of Europe, Brussels has become the most international and sophisticated city on the Continent. An astonishing twenty-five percent of its population is foreign, in large part made up of diplomats, executives of over 2,000 multinational corporations, and the military elite. I sat staring at the glorious caloric exhibition for a moment and heard the queen giggle.

"You're like my husband. He would make judgments of state in seconds but could never decide which pastry to choose."

"It's not indecision, Your Majesty. It's self-control."

"Surely you are not concerned about your weight, Miss Rhodes. You have a lovely figure."

"Thank you—but it's not the calories, it's the cousins."

Then I explained to her my tendency when confronted with a plethora of sublime confections to immediately snag a few of each. It's a technique I developed during my childhood in dealing with my four cousins from Long Island, who taught me a lesson in sibling survival that I as an only child had never needed to know. I learned that waiting to take a second piece of cake until you'd finished your first was dumb, since the entire platter would have been cleared off early on by kids who had learned to plan ahead. As they explained, you might never want that other slice, but the only way to insure that it'd be there in case you did was to put it on your plate at the get-go.

Dona Felippa threw back her head and laughed. She told me she was the youngest of six and was quite familiar with such family table tactics.

"Before you make the final fatal decision, Miss Rhodes," said the queen with a pretend-serious face, "perhaps you should first see these." She lifted the cover of a silver salver, and I made a deep sigh of pleasure as I inhaled the escaping delicious aroma.

"Would you perhaps like a hot waffle?"

Would I ever.

"Yes, please," I answered somewhat loudly to drown out the rumbling of my stomach, which hadn't had a visit from anything substantial since the seven-thirty a.m. roll and coffee. I'm a firm believer in trying *les spécialités de la pays* wherever I go and figure that if a whole nation loves it, it's worth a shot. Although I might make an exception if they offered me candied beetles; I'm intrepid, but my intestinal tract is not. The Belgian waffle was made famous at one of the U.S. World's Fairs, but why do things always taste better in their hometown? The usual Belgian waffle stall offers a choice of toppings, and many a blouse has suffered the consequences of my walking through a town square eating a hot waffle dripping with Belgian chocolate. There has always been a rivalry between Switzerland and Belgium over which country produces the finest chocolate, but true connoisseurs as well as discriminating chocoholics think the Swiss should stick to their yodeling.

Once we settled down to our eating, the conversation began to flow in all directions, and soon we were chatting away like old friends. We were now "Emma" and "Felippa," but, of course, I wasn't calling the queen Fab-baby. "Ma'am" was the accepted form of address.

When the queen mentioned how delighted she was to have Felippa visit her with the obviously adored little Juan, I thought it was time to bring up the topic I had been dying to touch upon.

"Why do you suppose those men were trying to kidnap Juan?"

My God. The last time I saw looks of such intense shock was when one of my breasts popped out of my décolletage at the Duke of Westminster's dinner table when I bent down to pick up an earring.

Felippa gathered herself together first. "For money, I suppose," she said with no conviction whatsoever.

"Is your husband a very wealthy man?" I had never heard of any Spanish noble who had made it big in the world markets, which was hardly surprising since generations of inbreeding usually blocked the entry of any significant brilliance into the aristocratic gene pool. And whereas the English lords managed to preserve their vast estates through progeniture, vast private Spanish land holdings were rare today. "By the way," I added, "where is your husband? I assume that you've told him about the situation."

The two women looked at each other in obvious terrible consternation, and suddenly Felippa burst into tears.

"*Felippa! Ni una otra palabra. Es peligroso.*"

Peligroso—dangerous!

"But I must talk to someone," she moaned. "*Tía*, she is so *simpática*."

There it is again—that talent I seem to have that makes people tell me things.

I don't know why—my face must project *simpática*, because often just moments after meeting someone, through introduction or merely casual encounter, he or she will start pouring out the kind of intimate life problems one usually reveals only to a best friend or bartender. Most of the time I don't really care. However, sometimes I do, and sometimes I do something about it. If they ask. And if they pay.

In fact, I make my living that way, and a fairly handsome one at that because monied people (I don't do pro bono) who are pulled out of the depths of personal misery tend to be very grateful, especially if the problem has been solved subtly, swiftly, and silently. Unlike the usual problem-solving professionals, shrinks and lawyers, who can only guarantee a protracted program of high hourly fees without any attendant assurance of satisfaction, I only expect payment if I am successful, and if the matter is settled within two weeks. I won't spend longer on anything because I have always suffered from Minimal Focal Faculty.

I made up that diagnostic term in high school to stop the constant complaints from head-shaking teachers and guidance counselors about how I was not working up to my full potential. Not that you could blame them. With my 165 I.Q., they expected great things, which can be a real pain when you're not interested in finding a cure for cancer or building the first Hilton on the moon. It's amazing how easy it is to sucker educators with psychobabble. Too insecure to admit their own ignorance, they instantly accepted my report of this mythical behavioral aberration as a bona fide learning disability. Thenceforth I got compassion instead of censure and was able to enjoy learning at my own pace.

Actually, the condition is real. All it means, in

plain English, is that I have no patience. Zilch. I was never one of those kids who labored and sweated for days on a project until it was perfect. If I can't get a handle on a problem within an hour, I'm out of there. My motto has always been if it's worth doing, it's worth doing well—but only if it doesn't take all day.

I like dealing with and working out people's problems. I am rather brilliant at it because I use the unorthodox tools of ingenuity, common sense, and a deep gut belief in my own infallibility. (Proven out, may I add, by a one-hundred-percent success record.) Did I mention that I have instant comprehension and superb insight? The fast-grasp feature I was born with; the understanding of human and often inhuman behavior I picked up during a lifetime of observation—that's twenty-five years of people-watching (I'm thirty-five, but I figure I didn't get too much out of the first ten years.)

My rather unique profession just happened because I have the insatiable desire to fix everyone's problems and the supreme confidence that I can. A chance heart-to-heart encounter with a woman on the hydrofoil going from Copenhagen to Malmö, Sweden, resulted in my extricating her from a very sticky and highly emotionally charged situation. She was enthralled with the results I achieved and insisted on paying me handsomely for my efforts.

I believe in the conveyor-belt theory of life, which is that we are all from time to time presented with passing opportunities, but only those with the brains to recognize the possibilities and the guts to act upon them are successful. Some people call it luck, but being in the right place at the right time doesn't mean squat unless you grab at the chance and go with it. When I looked at her check for just a week of effort and compared the hourly rate to what I got for the seventy-two-hour week I put in at the Wall Street law firm that enslaved me, a lightbulb went off in my head.

So I went into the business full-time. It is somewhat difficult to explain. I am like a P.I. in that I investigate private matters, but I take it a step further; I not only dig up the facts, I resolve the problems they have created. I am a P.R., Private Resolver. It's a profession that's all my own. I no longer try to explain what I do to people, because they immediately get that pitying look and the urge to take me out for a decent meal. They assume that I live in a seedy studio apartment strewn with my entire wardrobe of sweatpants and T-shirts, drive a twelve-year-old VW with no side windows, and subsist on a diet of Big Macs and Taco Bell takeout. What they do not understand is that my one-of-a-kind profession that's not listed in the Yellow Pages allows me to set the parameters. My terms are very simple: No up-front cash or per diems. I will devote two weeks to the matter and if I fail, you don't pay me a penny. But if I succeed, my fee is a flat $20,000, due immediately. It's the perfect proposition for the very rich who slaver at the chance to get something for nothing and adore risk-taking and gambling. Of course, I only deal with monied folk. Just as every girl's mother at some point told her that it was just as easy to fall in love with and marry a rich man as a poor man—that's how I feel about clients.

Which is why I have an apartment on Fifth Avenue in New York City, a flat on King's Road in London, and a casita overlooking the ocean in Vila do Mar, Portugal. I also have visiting privileges at the house where I grew up in Rye, New York, where my parents live when they're not in their Florida condo. They are the ones who taught me the value of money; I don't mean having it, I mean spending it. If I hadn't jumped off the mad success track with that million-dollar, multinamed law firm whose enforced seven-day workweeks of twelve-hour days gave me little time or energy to spend the big bucks they lured me in with, I wouldn't have been able to fly first-class, of course, to Belgium yesterday to take up the offer of an apartment in Brussels of friends who were vacating it for two weeks.

"Please, Felippa," I said, "if you have some trouble, perhaps I can help."

"How?" asked the queen. "You are a writer."

"Well, not really, Your Majesty. Actually, I make my living as a sort of personal private investigator."

They both looked at me in astonishment. I sighed. People always regard me dubiously when I make that statement. You can't blame them. What they see is a tall (5'6") woman with a size eight figure, long dark brown hair, huge brown eyes, and a face that has been called that of a sexy madonna (I mean the one shown in ecclesiastic paintings, not the aging self-proclaimed sex goddess of MTV). I have always ignored that I am considered beautiful but always have to deal with the fact that others cannot. It usually takes a bit of talking before they can get past that to realize that I have a mind. I also know that people would find it easier to accept my rather offbeat profession if I wore acrylic stretch slacks and a Macy's raincoat. Kinsey Milhone wears old jeans and turtlenecks and cuts her own hair with a cuticle scissors which gives her an aura of committed intensity, whereas my Calvin Klein jeans, violet silk Ralph Lauren shirt, Hermes scarf, and Kenneth-coiffed hair convey an image of a woman who divides her days between Bloomingdale's and Bergdorf's. I could never understand why all fictional private sleuths other than Hercule Poirot dress in schmattes, dwell in squalor, and wallow in poverty. Are the writers trying to convey that solving crimes demands a total dedication requiring one to abjure the niceties of life? It's not a calling, for God's sake, just a job. My life priorities are very simple—I work only to subsidize my very high style of living. And I don't see why I have to look like a bag lady when I do it.

I explained to them how I work, that I will only take on a matter if I feel I can bring it to a successful conclusion within two weeks.

"Since I don't get paid if I fail, I can't afford to handle situations that are out of my range of capability."

I mentioned my fee of *608,000 Belgian francs*, which they dismissed with a wave of the hand. But the two-week time limitation concerned them. How much could I cover in two weeks, just me alone, with no organization backup? I have never found a way to explain my abilities without sounding like a conceited twit. How can I tell people that my 165 I.Q. enables me to size up situations and analyze information almost instantaneously, and that working with lesser mortals would only slow me down? Unlike Sherlock Holmes and Hercule Poirot, I would find bumbling assistants a pain in the ass. I merely explained to the two women that I had found working solo to be the fastest, most efficient method of operation. And also the most discreet, since the only way to guarantee absolute secrecy was to involve no one but me. That's what did it.

Felippa looked at the queen and she nodded.

"We must have absolute secrecy, since my husband's life is at stake," she said emotionally.

"Absolutely," I said. "Now tell me all about it."

Felippa turned to me and the words poured out of her. "My husband is in hiding and I do not know where. I know why, but I do not know where!" she said in great anguish.

"From whom is he hiding?" I asked.

"A fanatic Islamic group called the Partisans of God. They are the same madmen who claim to have bombed the Jewish center in Argentina that killed one hundred people."

"But why are they after your husband?"

"My husband is an attaché to the Spanish embassy in Iran. He is also a brilliant archaeologist," she said proudly. "Last month, he was invited to give a series of lectures at the Hebrew University in Israel. It was a great honor—all the leading archaeologists of the world were there. A week after he returned to Iran, two leaders of the Partisans of God were assassinated. My husband was one of the few people who knew of the existence of this group; keeping track of terrorists was part of his duties. Those crazy men figured that Israelis must have done the killing, and since my husband had

just been in Israel, it must have been he who betrayed them. They announced they would seek
vengeance upon my husband. Fortunately, a colleague and friend got word of the vendetta and
warned Bernardo in time."

"Why wouldn't he tell you where he went?" I
asked.

"In order to protect me, he has let them know
through special channels that I am totally unaware
of his location. In that way, they will not try to
force that information from me. He feels it is best
that I truly do not know."

"Do you hear from him at all?" I asked.

"No. And I am frantic. I don't know if he's alive
or dead," she wailed.

Fabiola put her arms around her. "But, *querida*,
surely we would have heard. He must be all right."

"I wouldn't worry about your husband's safety
right now. The kidnapping attempt was obviously
to smoke him out of hiding, which means they
don't know where he is."

"You see?" the queen said happily.

"Why haven't you brought in the Spanish police? Now the Belgian police will also be involved
since the attempted crime took place on Belgian
soil."

"No, no!" Felippa said violently. "My husband
cautioned me not to. He said specifically to trust
no one in the police. We do not know the extent of
these terrorists; they have people and spies everywhere." Then she looked at me imploringly.
"That's why you are our only hope."

"There are two things to be done here—first to
prove your husband's innocence to that Islamic

group, and then to find him to let him know the
ban has been lifted." I thought for a moment. "I
think I may be able to help, but there are some
steps to take before I can commit myself."

"When will you let us know of your decision?"
Felippa asked anxiously.

"Tomorrow," I answered.

She smiled. "Somehow, I feel better already."

"And now, Emma," said the queen. "You must
be my guest at tomorrow evening's ball here at the
palace. The king is giving it in honor of his wife's
birthday."

"I'd love to," I said. "Then you must excuse me
now, Your Majesty. I've got to do some fast shopping. Ball gowns are not normally part of my packing when I travel."

"I'm delighted you can come." She and Felippa
rose. "My car will pick you up tomorrow at seven.
One of Inspector Heist's men should be ready to
take you home now." They smiled and left.

But it wasn't one of his men, it was the inspector
himself who came in.

"I thought I'd better come myself to help you
through the ordeal," he said.

"What ordeal?" I asked as he opened the door
to lead me out. Then I heard a tremendous uproar.

"The press," he said with a wry smile.

There must have been a hundred people—re-
porters, photographers, TV trucks—all screaming,
"Rhodes—Mees Rhodes!"

I turned to the inspector in shock. "What's all
this?"

He smiled. "You're a national heroine. You
saved the queen's nephew. Your picture will be all

over the front pages tomorrow and you'll be on every TV newscast."

I've spoken in front of large groups, I have dealt coolly with all kinds of emergency situations. But nothing could have prepared me for this screaming mob hurling questions and thrusting microphones in my face.

When he saw the look of alarm on my face, he stepped forward to the closest microphone.

"Miss Rhodes is naturally exhausted from her experience and would like to go home to rest. She has nothing more to add to the facts that I gave you earlier." He took my arm firmly and, as cameras clicked and whirred, fielded me skillfully into a car where I subsided in relief.

"Do they know where I am staying?" I asked.

"Certainly not," he said. "We would not want you bothered, and moreover, we would not want any friends or cohorts of the perpetrators to know where you live. Remember, you foiled their plan. I don't want to alarm you unnecessarily, but I just want you to be aware and careful."

I smiled. "Not to worry. I can take care of myself." But then suddenly weariness set in and I decided I have all day tomorrow to find a ball gown. Right now, a glass of wine, a quiet dinner, and stimulating companionship was what I needed. I looked at the inspector. This shouldn't be too difficult.

III

―――――――❧❦❧―――――――

"IT'S A GOOD thing I felt like dressing up tonight, Albert," I said (we were on a first name basis
now) as we sat on a banquette in the elegant turn-
of-the-century town house that was Comme Chez
Soi, the most expensive restaurant in all of Brussels.
There are only fourteen tables to amortize the owner's nightly expense of the huge crew of chefs,
whose activities are clearly visible through the
huge glass wall at the end of the room, which ac-
counts for the palate-pleasing food and the gut-
wrenching prices; I've never heard of a twosome
leaving there without having run up at least a
three-hundred-dollar tab. I had thought of wearing
jeans, expecting that an inspector's salary would
mean mussels, frites, and beer on the Rue des
Bouchers, which I dearly love. But flipping through
ELLE while soaking in the bath gave me one of
those image-changing yens that we women get
when we see how gorgeous a gal can be. So I opted
for sophisticated elegance and a little black Escada

number that elicited that satisfying wide-eyed look
that you know would have been accompanied by
a wolf whistle if your escort was less well-bred.

"You look lovely, but your beauty transcends
clothing," he said, tilting his head back and re-
garding me carefully. Then he leaned in close and
said, "In other words, Emma, you are a real fox."

I nearly spat out my marvelous Veuve Cliquot
champagne.

He looked at me in consternation. "Did I use the
wrong word?"

I laughed. "Not if this was 1970. I think you may
be watching too much old American TV."

"Well, the language may be dated, but surely the
meaning is timeless," he said, reaching for my
hand as I set my glass on the table.

My turn.

I left his hand where it was and then looked him
straight in the eye. "Your eloquence indicates far
more education than is required of a policeman,
your Turnbull-and-Asser shirt and Armani jacket
indicate disposable income not usually available to
a policeman, and you've taken me to a restaurant
that would put a serious dent into the monthly salary of a policeman. You're comfortable in your
skin, unlike a drug lord who has a fleet of Bentleys
but doesn't know which fork to use, so who are
you really?"

He smiled, and I noticed that he was one of those
eye-crinklers that I'm a sucker for.

"If we are getting into truth in identities, Emma,
then you have much to answer, but we can cover
me first. I am a graduate of the Sorbonne in philosophy. My father wished me to go on to the

Wharton School in America to prepare me to enter his world of business, but I disappointed him. I chose the police for my career."

"What's his business?" I asked.

"Now he is in the government—he is the Minister of Economic Affairs."

"And before that?" I asked.

He twiddled with his spoon and looked down for a moment. "My family has property. We own half of the Avenue Louise and a good part of the Meir in Antwerp."

The Avenue Louise is Brussels' Rodeo Drive and the Meir is Antwerp's Fifth Avenue.

Am I a good picker or what? It is said of Pamela Churchill Harriman by one of her "friends" that you could put a blindfold on her in a crowd and she would find the man of power. So it is with me, except my lure is money. I always seem to be drawn to men of wealth. It's not that I want any of the stuff, I have enough of my own. I'm not looking for what their money can buy for me, but rather what their money bought for them, like good education, manners, grooming, taste, and lovely teeth. I have a friend who distinguishes the nouveau riche from old money by teeth; her rationale is that bad teeth indicate a deprived background from a family unable to finance more than very basic childhood dental care. I'm not that nutty, but I have never been attracted to earthiness and I find grunge a real turnoff.

"First I will order," said Albert, "and then you will tell me all about you."

I had asked him to order for me. I find that an ideal tactic when a first-time date whose financial status is as yet unknown takes me to an expensive restaurant. Since I'm never sure that this isn't a gesture to impress and my skipping wildly through the table d'hôte could push him into bankruptcy, I play it coy and feminine and ask him to handle the whole matter. I just tell them no rabbit, since I raised them when I was a little kid and I do not like to eat anything I know socially. But no problem with my suave inspector—he skipped the prix fixe and went straight to the à la carte. We are in the gastronomic big time here.

By the time we had finished the renowned Mousses Wynants, which is a house specialty of roast goose pulverized to the consistency of whipped cream, Albert knew what I did for a living. I usually try to avoid dealing with local police since they're not happy with licensed private investigators, so you can imagine how they feel about unlicensed ones. But he was not your usual street-corner cop, and besides, I needed him. He had the two alleged perpetrators in custody and I wanted information, although I could not tell him why. I had decided the best route was to display interest in his prisoners strictly from the point of view of an involved party. I got around to it over our lobster cardinal.

"Are our two villains out of the hospital yet?" I asked.

"Oh, yes," he said, "bandaged but otherwise healthy."

"Healthy enough to tell you who they are and why they snatched that child?" I asked.

"They told us nothing—yet," he added. "We found Iranian passports in their room. Their fin-

gerprints came back from Interpol—they have records as small-time drug mules, nothing big. It's
puzzling, most criminals stick with their special-
ties, or their M.O.'s as they say on all your TV cop
shows. Why would they suddenly go into kidnapping? This is a sophisticated crime that takes planning and far more intelligence than these two idiots
possess. Also, the child is of a well-to-do noble
family, but there is no big money there."

"Could they be some kind of crazy terrorists?" I
asked innocently.

"We found some papers in their room about
something called 'Partisans of God,' but no one has
ever heard of them; they're not listed in our roster
of terrorist groups."

Bingo! Now I was ready to go home. From the
yearning look and the way he had been moving
around in his chair for the past five minutes, I
knew that so was he. But he was a gentleman to
the core.

"Would you care for a sweet?" he asked.

"I bet they do a marvelous Grand Marnier soufflé," I said innocently. His face dropped so drastically that I burst out laughing. "You'd make a
lousy poker player," I said. "I thought detectives
were impassive."

"But also impatient," he said. "Waiting the forty-
five minutes it takes for the soufflé to rise . . ."

"Might work conversely for you? Ah, I like a
man who blushes," I said. "But I'm ready—we can
have coffee at my place."

IV

HE WAS A lovely lover. After he left, it was almost midnight. A good time to reach my handy Israeli Intelligence friend. Abba spends his days doing unspoken-of and possibly unspeakable tasks and his nights socializing with a huge group of friends who love to talk, drink, and make love.

"Emma!" he yelled so loudly that I nearly dropped the receiver. "Where are you calling from, my adorable one, in Israel, I hope. It's a long time since I have made love to an American—they are afraid to come because of terrorism. Pfah! It is as quiet here as a tomb, or perhaps that's a poor choice of words."

I could tell he was in a roomful of friends and was speaking for an audience. Abba Levitar is five feet six inches tall and weighs about 250 pounds. I have never slept with him and the very thought makes me giggle. We have been good friends for ten years. I have given him the free use of my flat in London and my house in Portugal whenever he needs R&R from the searing demands of his job.

"At the moment, I need information, Abba, not sex."

"Wait while I switch phones," he said in immediate seriousness. After a few moments, he came back on the line with no background noises. "Now, what do you want to know?"

"Who is a group called the Partisans of God?"

He gave a loud hoot. "Those schmucks? They're not a group, they're a bunch of *charahim*, shitheads who like to play at being murderous terrorists but couldn't even close an open butcher shop on Ramadan."

Abba was born and bred in Brooklyn and has lived in Israel for the past twenty years. To mask his scholarly sensitive side, he affects a tough-guy patois of profanity which one merely accepts as part of his persona. I once asked him how come, though Israelis speak Hebrew, all their curse words are either Yiddish or Arabic. "Hebrew," he said, "is the language of the Bible. To curse in Hebrew would be blasphemy." Abba's Falstaffian manner masks a keen mind and intrepid courage that have moved him up through the ranks into one of the top positions in his very secret profession.

"But didn't they claim responsibility for the Buenos Aires bombing of the Jewish center?"

"*Everybody* claims responsibility when something big happens. Why not? All it costs is a phone call to the police, and then the fucking media people who are always looking for some *drek* to fill their pages report the call and *hutz-clutz* the group is famous with their name in the papers. Those Partisans of God are a pack of inept *idyotim* who couldn't blow up a pushcart."

"Then why did you assassinate two of their men a few months ago?" I asked.

This time I really did drop the receiver. His blast of laughter nearly shattered my ear and the phone. "Where did you pick up that *bubimiseh*? We wouldn't waste a *chatichat charah* on those dickheads, not a piece of shit in a slingshot."

"But they were killed."

"Yes, but not by us, I guarantee you."

"Then by whom?" I asked.

"I remember hearing they were involved in drugs to raise money for arms. Knowing that bunch, and we know them well, not one has the brains to run a falafel cart, let alone a drug operation. I would guess that a couple of those fuckers tried to play it cute with the big drug honcho who's behind it and were just squashed like the bugs that they were."

"Would you give me a written statement that Israelis had nothing to do with the killing?"

He laughed. "No way, *bubele*. We never declare or disavow responsibility for assassinations—after all, we're the arm of a legitimate government. We just keep quiet and let everyone make their own assumptions. You'd be surprised at how many murders have been incorrectly attributed to us. We like it. It's a good way of inspiring fear without costing us a man or a bullet."

"That means I'm going to have to find out who did kill those two," I said.

"You? Another one of your cases, Emma?" He was alarmed. "Listen, my darling *motek*, you're not

gentle Miss Marple in quiet St. Mary's Meade.
You're in the Middle East dealing with zealots and
drug criminals—the most dangerous combination
in the world. You don't need the money—forget
the whole case."

"Maybe you're right, Abba."

"Fuckin'-A I'm right," he said. "Keep out of it."

After I hung up, I sat back in bed and thought
about it. In all the private-eye books, this is where
the heroine becomes honorable and decides to continue the case purely on principle, even though her
life is in serious jeopardy and her financing has
been killed along with the client. This sudden con-
version to being Mother Teresa always struck me
as the thin device of a lazy writer who needs a
reason to keep the protagonist going after all valid
impetus has disappeared. Why should a cynical investigator who labors by the hour scratching out a
livelihood among a world of sleazebags suddenly
become inspired by a sense of justice to risk her
life, for free yet? It makes no sense, but the writer
is in a bind and has a book to finish. So the poor
reader has to suspend logic and blindly accept the
author's plot . . . much as we opera lovers have to
forget reality and blindly believe in the often out-
rageously convoluted turn of events that occurs on
the stage.

I despise injustice and will fight against it
wherever I can, but I'm not sure that I want to die
in the battle. I decided Abba was right and I would
tell Felippa tomorrow that I could not help her.
And I fell asleep with happy thoughts of shopping
tomorrow for a ball gown.

It was a beautiful cloudless morning when the

cabdriver dropped me off at Yves St. Laurent on Avenue Louise. As I walked toward the shop, he didn't leave but kept staring at me. I thought I had tipped him pretty lavishly, but who knew—maybe he'd been spoiled by the Japanese. I walked inside and a chic woman, who I later learned was the manager, greeted me with a smile. *"Bon jour, madame...."* Suddenly she stopped and gasped, *"Mon Dieu. Mais c'est elle."* It's her! Who? Two other saleswomen ran over, both saying the same thing. *"C'est elle!"*

What was going on? Noticing my stunned look, one of them brought over a newspaper—Holy cow! Guess who was on the front page? There was a huge full-page picture of me with an inset shot of little Juan! Full story inside.

"You are the one who saved our queen's little nephew. You are the brave heroine. Madame, you will be in our hearts forever." It was the kind of lavish language my mother used when she was president of the Rye Women's Club. The members lapped it up, but I always used to cringe into the folding chair.

After they finally calmed down, she showed me a few ball gowns. She asked where I planned to wear the dress and was enchanted when she heard it was for tonight's ball at the royal palace where I was the guest of Queen Fabiola. Every time I tried on another number, the entire staff would gather around and clap their hands with delight. *"Belle!"* "Exquisite!" *"Charmant!"* If this was a sales ploy, it sure was effective; I was almost ready to buy them all. However, reason prevailed. At $6,000 apiece, I figured one would get me through the rest of the year, especially since balls were not high on my social agenda. I finally settled on a light blue crushed velvet and tulle figure-clinging dress with darker blue appliqué bordering the plunging neckline, in which I must say I looked sensational. Luckily it needed no alteration so I was able to take it with me. I felt a little like Cinderella when I changed back into my jeans and walked up to the desk to pick up my already packed gown. I took out my credit card.

"Mais, non, madame," said the manager with a big smile. "Please, do not think of paying. We consider it an honor to give one of our gowns to our queen's benefactor and with it the gratitude of our nation."

I was stunned. Maybe there is something to this heroine business. My protestation had just the right amount of vigor to be polite but ignored. I was delighted to take the gift, but there were certain obligatory courtesies that had to be observed; it would be ungracious to take largesse without giving my benefactor the pleasure of convincing me of the importance of accepting her gift. I thanked her profusely and walked out feeling wonderful. My lightheartedness didn't last long. As I stepped out, I was stopped by a wall of people all screaming, *"C'est elle, l'héroïne!"* and camera bulbs began flashing. So much for altruism; obviously someone in the shop had alerted the press so that there would be a nice photo of me in front of Yves St. Laurent in tomorrow's tabloids. I guess her gift was more motivated by P.R. rather than patriotism. Oh, well, my mother always told me there's no such thing as free caviar. What the hell, percs are percs.

Finally a policeman had to break up the cheering

mob and help me find a cab home. As I walked in the door, the phone was ringing. It was Abba.

"Thank God I got you. Why didn't you tell me about your little crime-busting episode?"

"How did you hear about it?" I asked in surprise.

"Are you kidding? This is the land of David and Goliath. A beautiful young woman knocks out the big bad giant with a rock—who happens to be an Islamic terrorist, one of our favorite people—and you don't expect it to be on the front page of every Israeli newspaper? Of course, it would be better if you were Jewish. You wouldn't consider converting?"

"From what?" I asked. "You know I'm so unconcerned about religion that I don't even want to waste energy on being an atheist. Besides, I respect Judaism too much to insult it by ignoring it the way I do the religion imposed upon me at birth."

"Well, whatever you are not, one thing you are is famous all over the world."

"You mean I'm international news?" I asked in disbelief.

"You bet your sweet ass, baby—but I wish that's all that's at risk. Do you realize what you did with your little slingshot? You publicly shamed two Iranian males. Not only did you make them look like assholes by foiling their plan, but you committed the unforgivable sin of being a *woman*. To be beaten by another warrior has honor. But to be outsmarted by a mere woman is to make you unworthy and below contempt."

My knees felt weak and I sank into the chair. "What exactly does that mean?"

"The Mohammedan Macho method is vengeance. They can't rest until they dispose of you to regain their manhood."

"But they're in jail," I said.

He snorted. "For now! I don't know about the Belgian system and bail. But that doesn't matter—remember, the rest of their bunch is out there. Emma, you've got to disappear, and fast."

"For how long?" I asked.

"Maybe forever."

Then I got mad. "Those cruds are not going to make a Salman Rushdie of me. I'll be damned if some demented slimebuckets are going to drive me into hiding."

"Didn't you get what I said, Emma? They will kill you."

"Then I'll have to deactivate them first," I said firmly.

"How do you propose to do that?" he asked.

"With my brains. Look, you said they're a small, disorganized group. They now have two targets to go after, which has to cause some consternation and inefficiency in the ranks."

"What two targets?" Abba asked quickly. "Something else you haven't told me?"

I told him Felippa's story. I had no concern about his discretion, since secrecy is part of his life.

"So that's why you asked if we offed those men."

"Yes—and now I am going to take on her case. Before it was for money—but now it's for blood—mine."

"O.K., but first let's get you out of where you are."

"Why? No one knows I'm here." And then a sudden thought hit me. "I never gave you my phone number, Abba. How did you get it?"

"What do you think I am, Emma, a plumber? Which wouldn't be bad—they make more money than doctors and there are no night calls. I knew you'd rent a car, so I just accessed the computers of all the rental car agencies in Brussels. You have to give them your local address, so it was easy. Which is exactly why I'm telling you to leave fast."

"But I'm going to a ball at the royal palace tonight. Queen Fabiola is sending her car for me."

"All right—they don't have *yiddishe kopps* or sophisticated computers, so it may take those bastards a little longer. Here's what you do. Pack a bag and leave it right inside your front door and go to the ball. When you're ready to leave, tell the queen's driver that you won't need him because a friend is picking you up. Then call this number, say, 'leaving,' and go to the side door where a car will be waiting."

"Whose car?" I asked.

"One of ours. She'll take you to a safe place in Ixelles, not too far from where you are. We have a house there."

"What about my clothes?" I asked. Do I have my priorities right or what? Here he is talking about life and death and I'm worried about fresh underwear.

He laughed. "Just like a woman. And don't tell me that's a sexist remark; it's just a sage observation on realistic gender differences, courtesy of my psych degree from Brooklyn College. Don't worry—they'll be in your room when you arrive."

"I'm not going to ask you how you intend to get in here without a key. Diane and Bill told me proudly of the state-of-the-art security system in the building, but to your people, I guess it's child's play."

"You're right," he said. "Don't ask. To us, any building takes minutes. Fort Knox, a little longer. Now go off and have a good time. And yes, try not to stay much after midnight. Our people need their sleep. But never fear, you won't find a pumpkin outside if you're a bit late. But remember one thing—tell nobody, I mean *nobody* that you have left Avenue Hamoir. As far as anyone knows, you're still living at the same address. I'll talk to you tomorrow and we can work out some plans for your future to be sure that you have one."

"You sure know how to reassure a gal," I said with a laugh. "Thank you, Abba. I owe you more than one."

I hung up feeling totally sanguine. There's a saying that if everyone around you is losing their heads and you're not, perhaps you don't fully comprehend the situation. It's not that I don't know what forces I'm dealing with. It's just that I have complete confidence that I will find a way to right the whole matter. With my brain and Israeli Intelligence, how could we possibly lose?

V

———————❧❧———————

AS THE CAR approached, the royal palace looked like the fantasy in every little girl's dream. Like a glittering box, light streamed from all of the hundreds of windows as it did from the headlights of the long line of limousines moving slowly in to discharge their passengers. A huge crowd of people pressed up against the palace gates to watch the guests arrive and share in the festive aura of the gala evening.

When we arrived at the doors, a liveried footman escorted me out of the car and up the stairs, where he delivered me to another footman who took my invitation and announced me to the receiving line consisting of Queen Fabiola, King Albert, and his wife. Both queens were wearing diamond tiaras, diamond-and-ruby necklaces, and long white gloves.

"Emma, I'm so glad you could come," said Fabiola. She turned to her brother- and sister-in-law and said, "This is the brave lady I told you about."

King Albert, who had seemed a little stiff, broke into a big smile. "I hear you really trounced that villain."

"It really wasn't all that much. I just did what I had to do." Good Lord, I can't believe I said that. It's the classic folk hero cliché you hear on the six o'clock news out of the mouth of the fireman who saved the old woman, or the policeman who delivered a baby in the backseat of a car. This humble stuff is hard to handle; humility is a totally alien state for me.

"Emma, there you are."

I looked at Felippa gratefully as she drew me away and led me into the ballroom. The place was ablaze with light; I counted ten crystal chandeliers hanging from the gilt-and-ivory carved ceiling, not to mention the gold sconces along the walls. Waiters in gold-and-black livery moved among the hundreds of guests with silver trays carrying crystal glasses of champagne, and music was coming from the small orchestra on a platform at the end of the room.

Felippa gave me one of those quick woman-to-woman appraisals. "That's an Yves St. Laurent, isn't it? I almost bought it, but it was a bit too daring for me."

I looked at her Galanos gown that had no back and didn't say a word.

Her face became serious. "Have you decided?"

"The answer is yes, Felippa, but on one condition."

"Anything," she said fervently. "Name it."

"You must promise not to mention my involvement to anyone. I need absolute anonymity and secrecy in order to work freely."

Relief flooded her face. "I understand," she said solemnly. "You have my word." Then she looked around and said, "Come, there is someone you must meet. He is a close friend and a colleague of my husband. He is the one who warned Bernardo."

We walked across the room to a man who was talking to a bejeweled dowager. When he saw us approaching, I could see him excuse himself and walk toward us.

"Felippa, you look exquisite."

Talk about gorgeous, I nearly swooned. He was the exact replica of Tyrone Power, the 1940's Hollywood heartthrob.

"Emma, this is Don Luis Lopez de Lerma Avila. Luis, this is my friend Emma Rhodes."

"Ah, the heroine who is the talk of the Continent." He took my hand and actually kissed it—just like Tyrone Power.

"Oh, I see Tía Fabiola needs me," said Felippa. "I'll see you both later."

We stood and eyed each other silently for a moment.

"Why do I feel we're at Ascot inspecting the horses to determine which one will win the third race?" he said in that slowly drawn out, nasal upper-class English voice.

"I thought it was more like the au courant bar in Easthampton where we're evaluating the evening's offerings."

"Well," he said with a glorious smile displaying perfect white teeth, just like Tyrone Power, "like every royal ballroom, I would imagine this one has seen its share of male-female interplay throughout the ages."

"I thought the Belgian aristocracy were a rather sexually sedate crowd. I don't recall any Madame Pompadours or Lady Hamiltons peppering the history of Belgian court life."

"Perhaps that was due to maximum circumspection rather than minimal sexuality," he said.

"Now that we've finished with the conversational foreplay," I said, "let's get down to factual personal details."

"Fine. What do you want to know?" he asked.

"How do I figure a member of the Spanish aristocracy who looks like an Irish-American screen idol and speaks with an English public school accent?"

He threw back his head and laughed so loudly that neighboring heads turned toward us.

"You believe in direct action, don't you? Now I understand how you arrived at that astonishing but brilliantly simple response to a kidnapping in progress."

I accepted a glass of champagne from a passing waiter. "I find most problems have fairly simple solutions if you believe in your own intelligence. The trouble is most people don't trust their instincts, so they waste time reasoning when things could have been settled quickly with the one easy step they thought of first."

He raised his glass. "Miss Rhodes, I do believe that is profound. You are a philosopher as well as an activist. A rare combination in a beautiful woman."

"And I do believe you are trying to avoid answering my question about your rare combination of credentials."

"It's really quite simple," he said. "I am descended from one of the grandees of Castile. I was educated in Eton and Oxford where I was an Islamic scholar. As for looking like Tyrone Power, that has been one bloody nuisance; I cannot tell you how many elderly ladies stop me to demand my autograph."

"And do you oblige?"

"Of course," he said solemnly. "I couldn't possibly disappoint the dear old pusses by telling them he died years ago."

"Maybe seeing you for them is like sighting Elvis; it convinces them that their idol is still among the living."

"Well, they all seem to go off happy. Now what about you?"

I shook my head. "Nope, I'm not finished with you yet."

He hit his head in mock consternation. "Ye gods, this is worse than the orals for my doctorate. O.K., fire away."

"The Islamic scholarship—is that what brought you to the foreign service in Iran?"

"Yes. My family has been in the diplomatic service for generations, so it was the natural course for me to follow."

"What brings you to Brussels?"

I knew I sounded nosy, but I've never yet discovered a more efficient way to get information than to ask. There are those who enjoy drawing someone out, but I don't have the patience to play that game. Why spend hours of coyly worded hints and subtle directives to try to learn if the guy is worth two minutes of your time?

"My parents live here part of the year. My father is our King Don Juan de Carlos' personal emissary to the court of Belgium." He paused for a moment. "Has my interrogation been completed? Is it my turn yet, Miss Rhodes?"

"Emma," I said. "And may I call you Luis?"

"Of course. I think you and I would have a lot to talk about, Emma. But this is not the place. Have you ever seen Bruges? We have a lovely little house there where we could spend a quiet afternoon." Then he looked over my shoulder and said, "Oh, dear, it's as I feared. One can't monopolize a celebrity for long. There's a whole crush of people heading this way to talk to the heroine of the hour. Give me your phone number, please, so I can call you tomorrow."

Where? I thought. "I'm going to be in and out much of the day. Why don't I call you?"

He handed me his card and just before the group descended he said, "Tomorrow, please."

It was a glorious evening and I danced all night with many men, including my favorite Belgian inspector, who was there for security reasons. By twelve, I was exhausted and ready to leave. I located a phone and called the number Abba had given me and said the magic word, "Leaving," then walked out the side door fully expecting to have to wait, but a car was right there with a woman leaning against it. Obviously my call had been to a phone in a car that was standing by.

"Emma?" she called out, like a friend would.

I waved, walked up to her, and she embraced me as would a friend. And off we drove to my new home.

VI

~~~~~

IT WAS A white stone house set in a large garden.
I couldn't see much of the area at night, but ours
was one of the few houses with lights on, which
meant it was probably a quiet suburban neighborhood where residents turned in after the eleven
o'clock news. My driver, who had introduced herself as Esther Hirshon, took me upstairs to a large,
pleasantly furnished room. The wallpaper was pale
blue with small white flowers, matching the drapes
and bedspread. The furniture, consisting of a large
bed and dresser, was light oak with rounded corners in l'Art Nouveau style of the famous Brussels
architect Vincent Horta. My valise was on a luggage stand in the corner. She opened a door on the
side of the room.

"This is the bath," she said. "We have no other
guests at the moment, so it's all yours."

I plunked down on a pale blue wing chair. "I'm
very grateful for what you're doing for me."

She shrugged. "It's my job."

"You're a Sabra, aren't you?" She had that air of cool confidence, bordering on arrogance, that is the mark of the native-born Israeli who is justifiably proud of being part of a nation that achieved the almost impossible dream of creating a modern world out of a primitive, hostile land. She had un-made-up brown eyes, un-moussed curly auburn hair framing a face with high cheekbones, a strong straight nose, and that lovely tinged-with-copper skin that comes from spending years in the outdoors without sunblock. She was about my height and carried herself like a queen—another mark of the Sabra. She was not pretty, she was not beautiful, but she was striking. She was wearing the kind of loose brown jacket and skirt that is the instant I.D. of women who want you to know that they think fashion is trivial. The shapelessness couldn't mask her very trim lines and full bosom.

"Do you live here alone?" I asked.

"Just me and Martin, my husband." She told me that he was the head of European distribution for her father's engineering company. "Martin is a brilliant engineer and computer expert," she said proudly. "He's a graduate of your M.I.T." There was no mention of her connection to Abba's group, but I sensed immediately that she was a seasoned professional, which meant I would know only what little they thought I needed for survival.

She noticed me looking at the telephone and answering machine on a small table in the corner.

"That's yours. It's the same number as in your apartment in the Avenue Hamoir. We transferred it so that all your calls will come here."

The efficiency of Israeli Intelligence is awesome.

I believe that the incredible Jewish feat of surviving as a people over thousands of years of horrific injustices and oppression is due to a natural or developed genetic superiority in the brain areas that provide the traits needed to survive: intelligence, adaptability, and toughness. The age-old myth of them being cowards who eschew fights seems incredible in the light of the fact that the Israelis are regarded as the fiercest warriors in the world today. The possible explanation of this misconception is that they were never inclined to fight for nations which they knew were ever ready either to expel or exterminate them. Another could be the image of softness conveyed by their empathy for all victims of persecution. I have never been able to understand anti-Semitism, for that matter, any blanket anti's. Maybe because I was brought up to believe that each person bears responsibility for one's own life and actions, and blaming others for one's misfortunes may be temporarily comforting but ultimately counterproductive.

There was a knock and a tall, lanky, redheaded, red-bearded, bespectacled man stood on the threshold. "Hello."

Esther's face lit up and she walked over to kiss him lightly on the lips. She turned to me with the first smile I had seen on her face. "This is my husband, Dr. Martin Hirshon," she said proudly as he put his arm around her. He was a serious-looking man in his late thirties. "Darling, this is Emma Rhodes. She'll be staying here for a while."

We shook hands and said polite hello's. I noticed he didn't share his wife's careless attitude to appearance. His hair showed signs of a skilled razor-cut, and his beard was professionally trimmed. He wore chinos and a blue oxford shirt that were well-pressed, undoubtedly courtesy of his doting wife, and well-cut, I could swear courtesy of Eddie Bauer. I couldn't get too much instant insight into his character since his eyes were covered with rather heavy glasses, but he seemed pleasant enough.

"Why don't you come down and join us for a cup of tea when you're through unpacking? Esther makes the most wonderful strudel," he said, looking at his wife with a fond smile as she beamed back at him.

The phone rang and I looked at Esther in surprise. Who would be calling at this hour? I picked up the phone.

"Emma, darling, are you all right?"

I smiled broadly.

"Hi, Mom. I'm fine—how are you and Dad?"

Esther and her husband waved and motioned me to come downstairs, which I answered with a nod. They walked out and closed the door.

"We're fine, although seeing you on the six o'clock news gave us a bit of a jolt."

"Good Lord, the incident made it across the Pond?"

"It sounded a helluva lot bigger than an incident, Emmy Lou," said my dad, who was on the extension. Now my horrible secret is out—the name I was given to honor the memory of an aunt from the southern branch of my father's family. He has steadfastly refused to recognize my rejection of a name which to him conveyed charming images of fluttery femininity serving iced tea on the veranda and I considered a ludicrous label for a girl who climbed trees, played soccer, and beat up the block bully, Buddy Seiden, when he tried to play doctor. I proclaimed myself Emma after seeing Diana Rigg portray the daring Emma Peel in the English TV series *The Avengers*, a declaration my mother accepted immediately but my father has chosen to ignore.

"It really wasn't such a big deal," I said. "All I did was throw a rock at a bad guy."

"Did you really knock out the bastard from ten feet?" asked my father with what sounded very much like pride.

"Why are you surprised, Daddy? You're the one who taught me to pitch."

"I understand it was Queen Fabiola's nephew you saved," said my mother. "Did you meet her?"

"I just got back from a ball at the palace where I met her and the present king and queen." I knew this tidbit of information would get her off the phone fast because she had at least seven friends who would have to be called immediately to pass on the news.

"What were you wearing?" she asked.

I smiled. That's my mom. If I told her I was going to the guillotine, the first thing she'd want is a description of my outfit.

"This is where I sign off," said my dad. "Take care of yourself, sweetie. I love you."

"Bye, Dad. I love you, too. Mom, I wore an Yves St. Laurent ball gown that I bought yesterday."

"How much did it cost?" Of course the report would not be complete without the price tag.

"About six thousand dollars."

Now that she had all the important and impressive facts, I knew that farewell was imminent.

"Well, good night, dear. We're proud of you, as always. Keep in touch."

If I haven't mentioned it before, I'm crazy about my parents. If I ever murdered anyone, my lawyer could never get me off with the Menendez Mom-and-Dad-were-mean-to-me plea. It may sound unfashionable and uncool in this era of alleged dysfunctional families and suddenly recalled or fantasized familial abuse, but I had a great childhood and grew up basking in the unqualified love and approval of happily married parents. Sure, I had my little infracting episodes of minor rebellion, but I did not consider being grounded for a week an overly punitive response to my coming home from a high school party at five in the morning and puking what seemed like a gallon of beer on the front lawn. All in all, I fulfilled all their expectations and they fulfilled mine. I was valedictorian of my high school graduating class and had a near perfect average at Sarah Lawrence College. I went on to law school, worked for a posh law firm, and then quit to pursue a career doing they-are-not-sure-what to produce a high six-figure income. And they haven't bothered me with hints that she has a mother-of-the-bride dress waiting in the closet, or that he yearns for descendents to pass along the superb Rhodes' genes. Yet.

I hung away my gown and started to unpack my bag when the phone rang again.

"Emma, this is Albert. I didn't see you leave the ball. I have been calling, but your line was busy. Then I worried about who could be calling you at this hour of the night. Is everything all right?"

I sat down on the comfortable chair next to the phone to enjoy the conversation. Hearing him gave me that special lift I always get from hearing the voice of my man-of-the-moment.

"Everything's fine, Albert. That was my mom and dad calling from America. They saw me on the telly there and I just had to assure them that I'm O.K."

"Now how about assuring me?" he said. "The two men are safely locked away, and will be for some time. It's their associates who worry me. These are dangerous terrorists, Emma, and you have crossed them. I would like to assign a guard to you."

How do I get out of this one? I can just hear Abba if I tell him that his carefully inconspicuous secret safe house will now be distinguished by a patrolling gendarme.

"Unfortunately, Emma, my department doesn't have the manpower or budget to provide you with a guard. We're busy keeping watch over the little boy and Dona Felippa, since they are obviously in immediate danger."

What a relief. But let him worry. I've always found that a little guilt goes a long way in relationships.

"Albert, please don't be concerned. I'll be careful and I can take good care of myself." I could have added a small tremor to my voice to reinforce the picture of the brave lass, but I figured that might be overdoing it. I told him I would be out of town for a day or two and would call him upon my return. Then I unpacked, undressed, put on my favorite I-never-go-anywhere-without-it Viyella robe, and went downstairs to find the kitchen. It was easy—I just followed the delectable smell of hot strudel.

It was a warm, lived-in room that was obviously occupied by a serious cook. The cabinets and counters were white formica European hi-tech style, but the room was softened by the strings of garlic and onions and various cooking utensils that were hanging on the walls. Martin was sitting at the large round wood table in the middle of the room, and Esther was taking a steaming tray out of the microwave. When he saw me, he rose and brought the teapot to the table and filled the three mugs. Unlike Scarlett O'Hara, who always ate before attending the ball so that she shouldn't appear indelicately interested in food, I never eat before because I don't have a lady's maid like she did to squeeze me into my gown. When Esther placed the fragrant pastry on the table, they both started to laugh and she began shoveling a very large slice onto my plate.

"From the look on your face," said Martin, "either you're absolutely manic about strudel or you haven't eaten all day." He looked at me appraisingly. "I suspect it's a little bit of both."

I nodded my head, unable to talk with a mouthful.

"Then you must have some food," said Esther. "I can make you a sandwich . . . I have some brisket."

"My wife, the Jewish mother," said Martin, putting his arm around Esther. "Honey, I think you forget that it took two thousand years of wandering to develop the ability to digest brisket and strudel at one in the morning. For Emma's untrained gentile system, I think some bread and cheese would sit better."

I shot him a look of gratitude. And soon I was munching away happily on some marvelous Belgian bleu cheese and what tasted like home-baked four-grain bread.

We began to chat about Brussels and the people, and the tremendous activity caused by the European common market, and the wonderful restaurants. We soon lapsed into an easy relaxed relationship, which was rather remarkable since they, obviously well-trained, had managed to avoid asking a single personal question. Martin was highly intelligent with an acerbic wit and the rare ability to reproduce accents, which he used to entertain us with tales of the bumbling bureaucrats he dealt with daily at the EC. When he described them as "formicating functionaries," Esther turned pink. "Martin!" she said chidingly.

"Don't worry, Esther," I said. "I'm not offended. All he said was that they're a bunch of officials who run around like ants."

After two cups of tea, three slices of bread and cheese, two helpings of strudel, and an hour of stimulating conversation, my brain and body were crying for rest. Esther turned down my offer to help with the dishes.

"Don't bother, please, Martin will help me clean up. Won't you, darling?" she said mischievously. "He's an only child," she said smilingly, "and his mama spoiled him rotten, as you Americans say. But he's learning."

"It took me a year before I got over the habit of just leaving the table after eating. But now I've learned the error of my ways. I even wash pots," he said proudly.

I liked their fond bantering relationship, and apparently they did, too.

I went upstairs to my room, brushed my teeth, and fell into bed with two thoughts before I dropped off to sleep: (1) What a nice couple, maybe marriage was something I should seriously consider as a life option, and (2) what should I wear to Bruges tomorrow?

VII

WE WERE SITTING in Don Luis' house over-looking one of the lovely canals that weave their way through this medieval city. Whenever I visit Bruges, I expect to see Gene Kelly dancing through the streets, because the place is like *Brigadoon*—frozen in time. Actually, that is true, because in the 1400's this prosperous city, filled with palaces and elegant homes of wealthy merchants overlooking the canals, literally stopped dead and died, a victim of one of the strangest natural events in history . . . the "silting of the Zwin," the waterway that connected the city to the North Sea. For some reason, this estuary that was the basis of Bruges' prosperity began to fill with silt, thus making it unusable and impassable. How did the people handle this disaster? Very simply—they took off, leaving their houses and buildings intact. As a result, much of the city remains exactly as it was in the fifteenth century.

It's a marvelous walking city because it offers the

pleasure of coming upon sudden surprises. You turn a corner, and you're in a medieval courtyard where you expect to see Don Juan scaling the balcony. Just a few steps later, you come upon a canal bordered by houses with the unique Belgian architectural details of pointed roofs and bricks arranged in marvelous varieties of designs. And then there are the magnificent squares surrounded by belfries, guild halls, and town halls each decorated in golds, reds, greens, and blues.

We were sitting in a magnificent room that looked like a museum. Gold brocade drapes flanked the tall windows overlooking the canal. The chairs and sofas were covered in pale silk, and the wall facing the canal was floor-to-ceiling books, and I don't mean paperbacks; each leather-bound volume looked invaluable and read.

"Your family owns this house?" I asked Luis. "But what is an aristocratic Spanish family doing in Bruges? It's not a spa, there's no skiing, and there's no beach for miles."

"The house belonged to my mother's family," he answered. "She was born here."

"Your mother was Belgian? There had to be some Irish in her somewhere."

He looked astonished. "Her grandmother. How did you know?"

"Tyrone Power," I answered.

He looked at me in that casual-carnal way meant to melt the heart of any woman and the resolve of any virgin, if you can find one today. "I adore intelligent women." He smiled. "This is not a vacation home—but I do have a ski house in St. Moritz and a beach house in Morocco."

A beam of sunlight highlighted his head for a moment. God, he's positively gorgeous, Even handsomer than Tyrone Power, but no, that's not possible. We had driven down in his red Porsche in what seemed like half the time it took by train. I had him pick me up in front of the Yves St. Laurent shop on the Avenue Louise, where I told him I would be negotiating some alterations. I kept our traveling conversation light, but now I wanted to get down to basics.

"Is Bernardo's family like yours?"

"How do you mean?"

"Descended from the grandees of Castile." These were the upper crust of nobility in the sixteenth century and were actually called "cousins" by the king himself.

He said with pride, "Yes. Both Bernardo and I are descended from the original twenty-five families recognized by Charles V in 1520."

To be one of the original group was the highest social honor and prestige in Spain. As the centuries went on, the families may have become impoverished, but they firmly believed that nobility is an inherent quality which flows in the veins along with the blue blood and they would forever be superior to those who were merely granted titles for their services.

"Our families believe in honor, personal dignity, and self-sacrifice in the pursuit of higher ideals," he said. "Our emblem reads, 'Death less feared gives more life.' "

Gimme a break, I thought. If his family still managed to maintain this standard of living, then there had to have been some major business negotiations along the way in a world of high finance populated by thieves and sharks where the only sacrifices made are human ones, usually in the pursuit of higher deals rather than ideals.

Besides, the gap between ideals and reality grew wider with time, and Cervantes had Don Quixote deplore the fact that chivalry and knighthood weren't what they used to be: "Where is the knight now who would sleep in the open in all weathers with his armor about him?"

A true noble faces adversity though he may die in the effort. Don Bernardo's ancestors must be spinning in their mausoleums knowing that he fled rather than face death.

"I guess that's how you and Bernardo got to be friends."

"Oh, yes, we went to the same schools, parties— even loved the same women," he said with a smile.

"Felippa?" I asked.

He nodded. "Yes, Felippa. We both fell in love with her, but," he said ruefully, "she chose Bernardo."

Over this hunk? Maybe Bernardo looked like Errol Flynn.

"Felippa said you were the one who alerted him to the terrorists' threat."

He got up and walked around agitatedly.

"*Pobrecito!* This is not an enemy with whom you can stand up and fight. There is no fair battleground. They operate in stealth. You can't even reason with them. Bernardo did not want to hide— I convinced him it was the only way; for the sake of his family, he must save himself."

"How did you learn of the danger?" I asked.

"Dealing with terrorist groups is my department. As an Islamic scholar, I understand their language and mores. My job is to maintain a pipeline to their activities. One of my sources told me that these Partisans of God believe Bernardo is responsible for the Israelis killing two of their men."

"How did they know that Bernardo had been in Israel? And why do they believe the murders were committed by the Israelis?"

He threw open his arms. "Who knows?"

"Maybe they have their inside sources just like you do."

He shook his head. "I cannot believe that. Our security is excellent."

Words to live by—and die by.

"How long does Bernardo plan to drop out of the world?" I asked. "Salman Rushdie has been at it for years."

"Ah," he said, "but he doesn't have Emma Rhodes working to prove his innocence."

So much for Felippa's faithful promise that she would not divulge my role to a soul. I could just hear her protestations if I were to chastise her for breaking her word: "But Luis is a Spanish gentleman. He would never tell anyone." That's why I work strictly alone. I have learned that the sanctity of a secret is respected only by the individual upon whom the consequences of revelation fall.

"Did you know that the Partisans of God were involved with drugs?" I asked.

His face portrayed utter disdain. "No, but that doesn't surprise me. Those vermin would do anything to get money for their so-called cause, whatever it might be."

Suddenly he looked past me and his face registered surprise and then pleasure as he walked toward the door with his arms out.

"*Mamacita*—what a pleasant surprise!"

I looked at the woman who had entered the room and felt the frisson of pleasure one feels when coming suddenly upon startling beauty. It was instantly obvious where Luis got his looks. She wasn't tall, she wasn't young, but she conveyed an impact of statuesque ageless loveliness. Black hair with streaks of white at the temples worn simply with a center part and waves framed an exquisite face with the pale white skin and dark eyes that hinted of a black Irish heritage. She had the patrician poise that comes from an attitude of assumed eliteness natural to those born to power, position, or money. Her pale blue silk dress had the structured simplicity that indicated it was made for her figure at a cost of at least four figures. But that's not what impressed me; what got me was the casual elegance in which the Hermes silk scarf was draped around her neck. I've always marveled at women who can carry off scarf-wearing. I figure it's either a God-given talent or their lifestyles require no more strenuous activity than pouring tea. I've tried, but no matter how artfully I arrange my scarf in the morning, I find myself tugging at it all day and it literally becomes a pain in the neck. I have accepted the fact that my scarf-styling is limited to tucked in as an ascot or tied with the Girl Scout knot I learned to wear with my Brownie uniform.

"Mother—may I present Miss Emma Rhodes? Emma, this is my mother, Dona Isabella Lopez de

Lerma, Marquesa de Mantua." He kissed her warmly and his voice conveyed both pride and affection. I immediately liked him more.

I love happy family relationships. I'm weary of people who blame parents for their own failures and attribute all their vile personal behavior to Mom and Dad's psychologically damaging child rearing. Now it's entered the justice system as an acceptable excuse for patricide and matricide to the point where the old definition of "chutzpah" as a person who killed his parents and pleaded for clemency on the grounds that he was an orphan is no longer a joke.

Dona Isabella held out her hand to clasp mine and said with a delightful smile, "But of course, the brave lady who saved Juanito. How lovely to meet you." She looked up at her son with a roguish twinkle in her eye. "I can see that you didn't expect us. I'm sorry we did not let you know that we were coming, Luis, but it was an impulse of the moment. Your father and I felt quite suddenly that we needed a few days away from the demands of Brussels' social life."

Aha. So I am not the first woman who has been invited to the ancestral homestead. Mama's apology for her unheralded appearance indicated a familiarity with her son's assignation rites. Luis looked a bit shaken up by the interruption, but I heaved an inward sigh of relief that I wouldn't have to deal with any horny moves demanding delicate handling, since I had no intention of going to bed with him. This was strictly an educational visit for me, and his sexual skill was not in my curriculum. First place, he may be gorgeous, but he doesn't make my juices flow. Secondly, I already have a guy in Brussels, and I consider more than one man at a time to be arrant promiscuity. Hey, we all have our own personal moral codes.

"I've never been to Bruges and Luis kindly offered to show me the city," I said.

So I lied. Men love to be the one to introduce a woman to a first, and you can take that any way you wish. The role of instructor to the less-informed female makes them feel superior and encourages them to open up and talk freely. They get on a roll and lots of good stuff pours forth that gives you a swift education about what makes them tick, and that's what I wanted from Luis now.

"We were just about to embark on our little sight-seeing tour," said Luis. "I was planning to take Emma on a canal cruise and then lunch at one of the waterside cafés."

"That sounds like a perfect way to enjoy the beauties of our little city," said Dona Isabella. "You are fortunate in your guide, Miss Rhodes." She looked at her son proudly. "Luis is extremely knowledgeable—he had a first in history at Oxford and can tell you everything about the architecture and origins of not just this city but everywhere in the world. Did you know that he is the author of two books on Islamic history and that he is fluent in both Farsi and Arabic?"

"Like Cervantes, my son is a scholar, but not a businessman," said a deep voice as a huge, burly, somewhat fierce-looking man came into the room.

"Quite so, Father," said Luis with a smile. "But *Don Quixote* was first published in Brussels in 1607, and today everyone remembers Cervantes and loves *Don Quixote*. In three hundred years, who will remember you and love the software we manufacture?"

His father's roar of laughter as he put his arm around Luis indicated this was a dispute of long enough standing to have become merely irritating rather than corrosive.

"Father, may I present my friend, Miss Emma Rhodes? Emma, this is my father, Don Roderigo Lopez de Lerma, Marqués de Mantua."

His features were too irregular and coarse to consider him handsome, but the startling effect created by a shock of white hair over bristling black eyebrows and mustache made him striking. Before he leaned over to kiss my hand, his bright black eyes gave me the lascivious once-over that is as natural as breathing to every Latin male over the age of twelve.

"I may question my son's choice of career, but never his choice of women."

My two favorite national preferences for lovers are Irish and Latin men: Irishmen for their physical beauty and articulate charm, and Latins for their unabashed sexiness. Irishmen, however, seem to be better skilled at the courtship than the consummation, a situation that probably came about from years of sublimation caused by the hundreds of years of national poverty that forced men to delay marriage until they could support a wife while living in a rigid Catholic society that forbade premarital sex. None of this for Latin men: the only conversation they're interested in is strictly postcoital. Find a male with the eloquence of the Irish and the libido of the Latins and you have the potential for a memorable *affaire de coeur*. Luis was a case in point.

"She is not only lovely," said Dona Isabella, "she is also very brave. This is the young woman who saved Juanito."

Don Roderigo's eyes opened wide in astonishment and then did another quick head-to-toe reappraisal but this time without the lechery. "*You* knocked out that terrorist? I envisioned a woman like one of those Russian shot-put athletes."

"As I have often told you, Father, skill and brains often achieve far more than brute strength."

"If you have only just arrived," Dona Isabella said quickly, "then you have not had a chance to view our home, Miss Rhodes." We must be in sore-topic territory; she has the same let's-change-the-subject-before-it-leads-to-bloodshed voice my mother always takes when she wants to head off an argument between my dad and me.

"Please call me Emma," I said.

She acknowledged my statement with a tilt of her head.

"*Querida*," said her husband, "why don't you give Emma a tour while I talk some things over with Luis." He turned to me and added, "My son doesn't like to talk about our business, but I feel I must keep him advised because someday it will be his."

"And Silvia's," Luis added.

"Ah, yes, my dedicated daughter," he said. "Isn't Silvia planning to meet us here?"

"Yes, dear—she phoned to say she'll be along later."

"Well, this is turning into a regular family reunion—all that's missing is the Christmas tree," Luis said dryly.

Obviously his sister doesn't occupy the same loving spot in his heart as his parents. I can see that the waterside lunch he's planning for us will not be lacking in subjects of conversation. Since I'm an only child, I revel in tales of sibling rivalry. It relieves me to realize I didn't miss anything.

"Come along, my dear. Let me show you around while the men have their little chat."

We went through room after room of brocaded walls, crystal chandeliers, inlaid tables, and antique furniture that would made Sotheby's salivate. I have spent many weekends in stately homes that are furnished in this style; I enjoy the visits and admire the priceless heirlooms. But live among them, never. My first action if I owned such a home would be to install a humongous electronic vacuuming system that would suck centuries of dust out of the place. The result would probably be instant disintegration of draperies, Oriental rugs, and wall hangings which are undoubtedly now held together by years of accumulated dirt.

Dona Isabella told me that although most families abandoned Bruges at the time of the silting of the Zwin, there was a revival of sorts in the seventeenth century when her ancestor built the house. It had been in the family ever since, and as the only child of the last descendant it became hers. Her great-great-great-grandfather had married a Spanish noblewoman and the family became Spanish entwined with Belgian.

"It was through our family that Fabiola was introduced to Baudouin," she said with a proud

smile. We were in a magnificent bedroom that was
the size of my entire King's Road flat; it had three
crystal chandeliers, four sofas, countless end tables,
and a silk-canopied bed. I stopped at one table and
stared at the small drawing that was standing on
a gold easel.

"You like my little Picasso?" she asked.

"I thought I knew all of his group of musician
sketches. It's wonderful."

"My father gave that to me when Silvia was
born. His instructions were that I was to give it to
Silvia when she had her first child."

As we walked back down the lovely curved
staircase, Dona Isabella stopped and stiffened.
"Cigarettes! Silvia is here."

She was stretched out on one of the brocade sofas with her face swathed in smoke. Luis and his
father were standing nearby, and the emotional climate in the room had dropped considerably.

"Put that out at once, please," said Dona Isabella.

Silvia sat up languidly. "Oh, yes, I forgot," she
said, "our precious fabrics and antiques." She
looked around for a nonexistent ashtray and then
made do with a small Imari dish that probably cost
enough to keep her in cigarettes for a year. She
suddenly became aware of me.

"And who's this? Let me guess—one of Luis', er,
associates."

Luis looked at me with a slightly reddened face
and I think was about to disabuse his sister of the
notion that I was just another of his bed 'n' Bruges
bimbos, but I headed him off because I often find
that people tend to speak more freely when they
discount you in the intelligence department. There

are women who have built fortunes on such misconceptions. Under the black roots of many a dumb blonde resides the shrewd brain of a Wall Street wizard. If you question this fact, just check out the financial statement of Ivana Trump.

I held my hand out. "Hello, I'm Emma Rhodes."

Her eyes narrowed. "You're American. You look familiar. . . ." Her eyes widened. "You're the woman who beaned that Arab who was trying to snatch Juanito."

"I should have sent you to finishing school instead of the Harvard Business School," said Don Roderigo, shaking his head ruefully. "That American slang is not becoming to a lady."

"You didn't send me there to become a lady— you sent me to learn how to run our business like a man since there was obviously no one else in the family to fill that role."

I bet at this moment Luis wishes he was an only child.

She eyed my beige linen Jones New York pants outfit and said, "You look like you're better at throwing parties than stones."

Honey, I thought, you're out of your league.

"It's all genetics," I said sweetly. "I inherited my father's pitching arm just like you inherited your father's looks."

When it comes to teaching someone a lesson, I believe in the one-step school of emotional laceration: head right for the jugular and be done with it. To be the unattractive daughter of a beautiful woman is one of the greatest curses that can be inflicted upon any girl. Silvia's shift from derision to distress showed that I had hit the mark. The large frame and coarse features made her father an imposing attractive man but gave Silvia the look of a prison matron. Hitting on her sensitive spot may seem a tad mean, but I was restrained. I could have said if her mustache were just a little bigger she would have been the spitting image of her dad.

The phone rang and the maid came in to announce, "*C'est pour Ma'mselle Silvia.*" Silvia picked up the phone in the next room and we could hear her speaking rapidly in Farsi. I speak a number of languages, Farsi not being one of them. But for some reason, I have picked up the numerals in almost every tongue, which is why I noticed Silvia's frequent allusion to "*bist-o-panjum*" which means twenty-fifth.

"My children are obsessed with Islam, Señorita Emma," said Don Roderigo, shaking his head. "The Moors figured prominently in Spanish history, so who knows, perhaps there is some ancient Moorish blood in our family."

"My interests are career-driven, Father. Silvia's are, I think, more social," said Luis.

When Silvia returned, I commented on her fluency in Farsi and asked what interested her enough to study such a difficult language. Her brusque answer was that it was useful in business. I decided it was time for a cease-fire; hostility is always counterproductive, and besides, Silvia had started to interest me.

"I understand you run the business, Silvia. That's great. One of the best things coming out of the women's movement is that it's become just as customary for fathers to turn businesses over to daughters instead of only sons."

She softened a bit and smiled for the first time, and what a change that made; once the sulky sneer disappeared, her face looked almost pretty. Maybe I'm pushing it—I'll settle for "attractive."

She began to talk enthusiastically about the British company they had acquired five years ago which, under her stewardship, had quadrupled its net income. I know quite a bit about software, not just from being a computer nerd, but more from having been involved a few years ago with one of the largest software companies in the world. Actually, my connection was more with the CEO than the company, but with people at that corporate level their business is as basic as breathing and even pillow talk can consist of market share and mergers.

When Silvia noticed that my questions displayed knowledge and sincere interest rather than social politeness, she opened up and became animated. The company was located in High Wycombe, where she spent most of her time.

"That's near West Wycombe, isn't it?" I asked.

"Yes," she said, "in fact, that's where I live. I have a house there."

"Not one of those glorious seventeenth-century cottages on the High Street?" I asked.

She smiled with pleasure. "Just off the High Street."

She was pleased at my familiarity with the area. Actually, it's one of my favorite villages in all of England.

"In fact, I'm going there the day after tomorrow," I said.

Luis looked surprised. I hadn't mentioned the

trip because the plan was two seconds old.

"Then you must visit me," said Silvia. "I'm going there tomorrow and will be there all week."

God, I'm good. Here I'd thought I might have to work at it for an hour to wangle the invitation.

Dona Isabella was smiling benignly at both of us, obviously delighted to see harmony. Given the prickly disposition of her daughter, I don't guess she sees too much pleasantness in the parlor when Silvia is around. "Why don't we go up to my sitting room to have a just-girls chat and leave the men to their business?"

Silvia and I winced, and she was about to make some sharp feminist comment when I caught her eye and shrugged with a smile. She grinned back at me and we followed her mother out of the room.

Dona Isabella kept showing me baby pictures, which embarrassed Silvia but I happen to enjoy. It's fun to see people you know in the pupa stage and spot nascent qualities. Luis had been gorgeous always, but poor Silvia was a klutz from the get-go.

I noticed portraits in mortarboards.

"My children were excellent students," Dona Isabella said proudly. "Both were graduated from Oxford University."

"Oh, Mama, I don't think Emma is interested in our school days," said Silvia.

"Oh, but I am," I said. "What did you study?"

"Theology. Of all religions."

"Is that when you first became interested in Islam?" I asked.

She shot a sharp look at me. "As a matter of fact, yes. I read some of the books on Islamic history and Persian poetry that my brother brought home."

Dona Isabella walked across the room, and I saw Silvia's eyes following her with a look of love and such utter desolation I almost had to look away. The mother had an almost translucent beauty plus innate grace and charm; none of it had been passed on to the daughter, who must suffer the lack every day of her life. I began to feel very sorry for Silvia.

"There you all are, my ladies," said Luis as he stood at the doorway. "Come, Emma, if we don't go now, we'll miss the beauties of Bruges in the sunlight."

As we walked out, Silvia handed me her card. "You won't forget to visit me in West Wycombe, will you? You needn't phone—just come. I'll be at home for a few days because I'm having the decorators in."

I assured her that I will be there. I had the feeling that, away from her family, I will find a very different Silvia.

Luis and I sat outside at a table at the Restaurant Den Braamberg, which is located right off the Rozenhoedkaai, a picture-postcard spot of intersecting canals. We sipped a lovely dry white wine, which accompanied grilled sole fresh out of the North Sea, a pile of frites, and a large salad. I have a number of friends whose idea of heaven is crisscrossing Lyons to visit every haute cuisine establishment in the area, which I call the four-star route to a quadruple heart bypass. I enjoy and appreciate the artistry of fine cooking and classic sauces, but for sheer contentment during and after the meal, I prefer to dine on simpler fare.

It was peaceful, just talking and watching the boats and swans go by on the canal when suddenly Luis looked at his watch and sat up. "Please excuse me, Emma—I must make a call." And he whipped a phone out of his pocket.

The one who invented cellular phones has a lot to answer for. The newest form of urban irritation on buses, trains, or just walking the streets are the loudmouths who make us unwilling listeners to the boring details of their lives or businesses. I would like to lock the cellular phone inventor in a room with the person who invented voice mail and let them kill each other by a new way to die, telephone torture.

I sat there, mildly annoyed, especially since I couldn't even have the pleasure of eavesdropping because he was speaking Farsi. Again I heard *"bist-o-panjum"*—maybe the twenty-fifth was a big Iranian holiday.

He hung up and motioned to the waiter for the check.

"I'm afraid we have to end this idyll, my dear," he said, putting his hand on mine and giving me that soulful and sexy straight-in-your-eyes look. That Latin-Irish combo is hard to beat. "Unfortunately, I have an important meeting in Brussels this evening and I must get back."

We tooled along in his red Porsche, this time at less than Le Mans speeds, feeling that wonderful mellow all's-swell-with-the-world sense one experiences after a satisfying day. Then I heard a loud roar and turned around in irritation to see what hotshot was polluting my peace.

"Luis, there's a car bearing down on us."

He looked in his rearview mirror. "What is he doing? This is just a two-lane road. The idiot can't think to pass me. One of us will go over the side for sure."

He accelerated but not in enough time before the car came closer along my side and I saw the gun.

"Luis, he's got an Uzzi." I was too stunned to be frightened as I saw the barrel swivel toward me. I heard two loud noises and watched the gunman's head explode along with the driver's. Their car veered off the side and we heard it crash below. Luis stopped, as did the car that had come up behind us. Esther stepped out, tossed her Uzzi into her car, and came up to us.

"It's a good thing I happened to be in the neighborhood," she said laconically. "Why don't you two leave? We'll take care of things here." I noticed a man getting out of her car and looking over the side.

Luis sat still, totally stunned. Before he could say anything, I said, "Luis, please start the car and take me home."

"What just happened here?" he asked, bewildered. I couldn't blame him. Things had moved pretty fast.

"Please, Luis, let's get out of here!"

He started the car and we drove for a few moments.

"Who the hell was that?" he asked.

"Just a masked man who happened to be passing by," I said.

"She knew you."

"Yes, she's a friend."

He eyed me narrowly. "You have some unusual friends. She just saved our lives, you know."

Not "our" lives, honey . . . that gun was pointed directly at me.

I smiled. "What are friends for?"

We drove back to Brussels in absolute silence. He dropped me off at Avenue Hamoir only after I assured him I would lock all doors and windows. Then I called a cab to take me to my safe house. I walked in to find Esther in the kitchen slicing onions.

"I assume those tears are from the onions, not for those two men back there in Bruges."

"The only ones who will shed tears for those murderers are their mothers," she said calmly as she kept slicing. "It was a good thing you left that note saying where you were going."

"I'll say. Thank you, Esther, very much."

She shrugged. "It's my job."

"Who were they?"

"They carried no papers, of course. But I recognized them, two fanatics from that ridiculous group the Partisans of God. The question is, how did they know you would be there? Who knew you were going to Bruges?"

"You, me, and Luis," I said.

She looked at me and then dropped the onions into a boiling pot.

"Maybe they followed me," I said lamely.

"You would have noticed them. Bruges is a small town."

"I didn't see you, Esther, and you followed me."

She looked at me scornfully. "Of course not. First, I know Bruges very well, and second—I am a trained professional. Those two are just stupid thugs."

We heard the front door open and Martin walked in. He looked a bit startled to see me there, and then went over to kiss Esther. As they embraced, she looked over his shoulder at me and gave a slight warning shake of the head. Was she telling me not to mention the day's little roadside fracas? Does that mean he doesn't know what she does?

"He knows," she said later, after he had gone upstairs to shower and change and we were sitting at the table having tea. "Well, maybe not every little thing," she added. She explained that Martin and she had met while serving in the Israeli army. "He was very brave, very smart, and he speaks Arabic and Farsi," she said proudly. "As a result, he was sent on many secret missions and caught the eye of the Mossad, which he joined after his conscription was completed." She stopped suddenly and was silent for a moment. "He was a rising star there; he could have become a true hero for our country."

"What stopped him?"

She looked saddened. "Martin is a Sabra, but he never had the soul of a pioneer as we all did. His priorities have always been more personal."

"But he seems so much to be such an activist, the kind who would be driven by a cause," I said.

She smiled ruefully. "The only cause that drives Martin is money. I never cared about possessions or wealth, maybe because I always had it. My father has built one of the largest engineering companies in Israel and we always lived well. But Martin's parents had very little money. They were piano teachers, highly respected but poor. Perhaps if Martin had been raised in a kibbutz where everyone exists at the same economic level, he wouldn't have felt deprived. But they lived in Tel Aviv, where financial differences were more readily apparent. So to Martin now, to reach a high level of wealth is important."

"I've often wondered how living at the low end of an upscale community affects kids," I said. "I grew up in a very affluent area where I saw parents drive themselves to support a home they really couldn't handle in order, they said, to give their children the benefits of a rich town and being able to associate with the so-called 'right people.' But how did those kids feel about not being able to afford the luxuries their friends took for granted, like five-speed bikes, designer jeans, new cars, country clubs in the summer?"

"I think," said Esther, sipping her tea, "if they were taught the right values at home, to understand the greater importance of ability and character and to feel a sense of pride in achievement in areas other than moneymaking, these differences wouldn't matter. If a child is taught to appreciate his or her own self-worth and thus becomes a whole person, he or she is invulnerable for life."

"Yet Martin seems like such a strong and directed person," I said, "and for two people with differing goals, you seem to be a very harmonious twosome."

She smiled happily. "Oh, we are—he's a mar-

velous, loving husband, and he's very happy working for my father. He quit the Mossad when we
became engaged and joined my father's company.
He was given the entire continent of Europe as his
territory and is doing wonderfully. I'm an only
child, so someday Martin will probably take over
the business. I just hope he's not too impatient,"
she said with a laugh. "My father is a young fifty-
seven who just married his third wife."

"But you didn't quit the Mossad," I said.

"No." She waved her hand in a self-deprecating
gesture. "But now I only do little things for them,
most of which Martin knows about. Like providing
safe houses for Abba's people."

"But not that you're in the business of removing
people?" I said. She nodded. I call packing an Uzzi
more than a small thing. But then, I guess mores
of marital trust differ. The French consider discreet
adultery acceptable. I guess Esther feels the same
way about killing. Assignations, assassinations—
what's the difference as long as they're performed
with circumspection? Maybe marriage isn't for me
after all.

I had to let Esther know where I would be for
the next few days. I wrote a note giving my London address and phone, and what methods of
transportation I would be using, and dropped the
note on the hall table. Then I went up to my room
and took a bath. I always think well in the tub; not
only am I cleaning my body but clearing my head
so it can work methodically to reach a conclusion.

Only Luis knew I would be in Bruges. Luis has
links to the Partisans of God and also to Bernardo.
Why would he want to direct their ire to Bernardo?

Could it be that he is still very much in love with
Felippa and wants to (a) punish Bernardo for getting the girl or (b) get rid of Bernardo so that he
has a chance to end up with the girl? And how can
Tyrone Power be anything but the hero? Well, at
least I've completed half of my assignment; I know
where Bernardo is hiding. Now all I have to do is
find out who really committed the murders attributed to him and advise the Partisans of God. The
phone rang and I figured I'd let the machine take
the message, which I could hear through the bathroom door. The urgency of the tone made me wrap
myself in a towel and run out to pick up. It was
my inspector.

"Emma, I just called to see if you're all right. I
want so much to see you, but unfortunately the
case of Juanito's attempted kidnapping has tied up
the Judiciaire so that I cannot get away tonight or
tomorrow."

Since I planned to be in England, I wasn't too
heartbroken. I told him where I was going.

"Please be careful, Emma, you must not forget
those terrorists want to harm you." There was a
slight silence. "If anything happened to you, I
would be desolate."

Now that's the kind of talk a woman loves to
hear. I felt a rush of affection for him. I assured
him I would be ever watchful and would phone
him upon my return. Fortunately, he was too pre-
occupied to question the reason for my trip, which
meant I didn't have to make up one of those imag-
inative cover stories that I've become so good at.

Albert knows what I do, but he doesn't have to know exactly how I do it. Every profession has its creative side—did you ever hear a doctor answer a question like "When will my back get better?"

VIII

I TOOK A taxi from the Gare du Midi station to catch the Eurostar Train that would take me to London's Waterloo station in a miraculous three and a half hours, thanks to the Channel Tunnel. Initially, I had been leery about taking this mode of transportation. I like to use the latest state-of-the-art developments, but the idea of riding underwater for three hours didn't thrill me. I'm not phobic, just pragmatic. Moses might have been able to keep the sea away, but I don't know about English and French engineers. I would find it difficult to sit in the dark for three hours worrying if ordinary men can build a structure reliable enough to keep the English Channel off my head. I read the BritRail brochure and nowhere in its glossy pages did I get any reassurance. Then I thought of phoning Diane Reed in the U.S., my Brussels hostess who I knew had taken the Channel Train a few times, and asking how she survived the underwater sequence. "Three hours? No way. You're above-ground for most of the trip . . . the underwater part is only about twenty minutes. It's no different than riding the subway."

No wonder the Channel Tunnel is in trouble. The first thing they ought to do is get rid of their advertising people. If any of those brilliant creative minds had bothered to have a few Focus Groups, they would have undoubtedly learned that most of the public thinks as I did. And instead of the innocuous headline of their brochure that says, "London to Paris or Brussels in about three hours . . . speed . . . comfort . . . convenience," which does nothing for normal claustrophobia, it would read in big bold letters, "INCLUDING A SHORT TWENTY-MINUTE RUN THROUGH THE NEW CHANNEL TUNNEL."

It was a marvelous trip. I went first-class, of course, which cost about 7,500 Belgian francs. The sense of feeling special starts at the Midi station where you find yellow-and-navy uniformed attendants waiting to help you through ticket purchases and passport checks. The setup is much like an airline check-in for luggage except here you must affix a tag to each piece identifying your name, car number, and seat. I was guided to my seat by one of the many attendants and immediately offered a drink and a menu. The food and drinks were surprisingly good and the service was excellent. The tracks in Belgium are not yet ready for high-speed trains, so we went normal speed through Belgium, which was lovely because it gave me a chance to enjoy the verdant Belgian countryside. When we reached Lille in France, we hit 180-miles-an-hour speed, and the twenty minutes of underwater darkness went quickly. What with food, two Bloody

Marys, and a small snooze, I was in Waterloo station in no time and in my London home fifteen minutes later.

My London flat is a pied-à-terre. It's not opulent but it's comfortable, spacious, cheerful, and wonderfully located. Part of a block of flats atop four floors of offices on the corner of the King's Road and Sidney Street, it's directly opposite the Chelsea Town Hall and Library, which besides filling my omnivorous reading needs, hosts marvelous antique shows and special events. It consists of a living room, kitchen, bedroom, and bathroom, and has sliding glass doors in the living room and bedroom leading to a huge terrace where I sit on Sunday mornings reading my favorite newspaper, the *London Times*. I've tried to dress it up with one of those great penthouse gardens I always read about, but I'm not there for predictable periods and things seem to turn brown when I'm there and bloom when I'm not. The woman who comes in to clean every week assures me she waters religiously, which probably means she clutches her crucifix while wielding the watering can, since the shriveled plants do not support her allegation. The place is furnished simply, mostly from the Habitat store downstairs. Beige wall-to-wall carpeting throughout, including the bathroom (I walk around barefoot and prefer warm rugs rather than cold floors; the more elegant Oriental rugs on polished parquet are part of the decor of my larger New York apartment), soft peach drapes, and comfy goosedown-filled couch and chairs, a very comfortable bed with fine percale linens, and a well-equipped kitchen provide everything I need for my drop-in visits. Including today's communications necessities—each of my three abodes has an answering machine, computer, and fax.

The location is ideal. Six different buses stop on the corner and taxis are constantly running by. Waitrose, an upscale supermarket purveying a myriad of superbly prepared foods ready for the microwave plus a selection of nonvintage *vins de pays* that suit my peasant palate, is but a few doors down. My years in Portugal where I lived on Dao and other simple delicious native wines have made me scorn the cork-sniffers who have to pass judgment on each bottle with the portentous gravity of a magistrate debating the prisoner's fate. A laundry that offers two-hour delivery is down the block. You can get a pretty fair ploughman's lunch at the pub around the corner, and I'm only four blocks from the Chelsea Kitchen that offers a crusty beef-and-kidney pie surrounded by a mass of crisp chips and veggies for just five pounds, and fish-and-chips with sprouts for only two pounds eighty. It's not that I can't afford pricey exclusive restaurants, it's that I prefer simpler eating and informal ambience. The Chelsea Kitchen puts you at any table that has an available seat, which can result in dining with some weird chaps as well as some very interesting people. It's an adventure and I'm always up for that.

I flopped down on my couch when I arrived. Travel days are always exhausting. Then I went into the kitchen and popped a Waitrose Chicken Tikka Marsala into the microwave and opened the chilled Chardonnay that Jim had placed in my fridge. Jim is the concierge of the building who takes care of my flat during my absences. He pays the cleaning woman, the TV taxes (You pay a tax to the government if you own a TV. Vans with electronic detectors roam the streets constantly to check on the existence of rogue TV's and you get hit with a thousand-pound fine if caught.), and fills the fridge for me before I arrive. Jim is the counterpart of Tom, the doorman in my New York apartment building, and Gloria in Portugal. They are invaluable and necessary aides for absentee owners and are worth every dollar, pound, and escudo I pay them. After dinner, I watched a bit of English TV— their sitcoms are usually dreadful except for a few like *To the Manner Born* and *Yes, Minister*, but they are masters of mysteries. I got lucky and sat up until eleven with Inspector Morse.

Something woke me out of a sound sleep. It was a noise on the terrace, like a scratching at the closed glass door. It must be those damned pigeons again; I'd better shoo them away or their cooing will keep me awake all night. I got up, drew open the drapes, and came face-to-face with a black-bearded man with a large knife in his hand. Yes, I screamed— wouldn't you? But he didn't make a sound as he suddenly crumbled to the ground. I stood there stunned as a tall young man with an Israeli *keepah* on his head and a truncheon in his hand bent over and calmly hefted the body over his shoulder and waved to me with a smile as he swung his legs over the side of my terrace and disappeared from view. I headed for the kitchen to make a cup of tea but changed my mind and poured myself a stiff snifter of brandy.

You can have your fairy godmothers—I'll take

the Mossad every time. Who knew I would be in London? When I thought about it, I realized—everybody. Luis and his entire family, even their maid. She spoke French, but she might also speak English. Now I'm getting paranoid. I have to get this case worked out faster than the usual two weeks before I turn into a "me" I don't like.

IX

SUDDENLY I WAS in the fifteenth century. As I stood at the top of the High Street of West Wycombe Village, I looked at the slightly crooked upper stories and century-old chimneys of the tiny timber-framed brick cottages that have undergone no external changes since they were handcrafted in the 1600's, and I felt like the hero of Jack Finney's classic back-in-time epic, *Of Time and Again*. There has been a village here for at least one thousand years—and I am there.

It was a quiet sunny morning, luckily devoid of the large lorries that break the spell of enchanting timelessness as they lurch noisily along the narrow road originally built for horse-drawn carriages. I take a day trip to West Wycombe whenever I'm in London. The Oxford train from Marlybone station gets you to High Wycombe in forty minutes, and then a ten-minute bus or taxi ride drops you off in the village.

I've developed my own special walk to savor the

sense of awe I always experience in the presence of historic reminders of the far earlier existence of people like us. I start at 21 High Street, which was a fifteenth-century rest house for pilgrims on their way to Oxford, and touch the wooden post that once held a large crucifix and the boulder below that was the knee-rest of the devout. The building is used today for town meetings and good-cause fund-raising events. Across the street is the Swan Inn (reputed to have its own ghost) and further along is the Unicorn Inn, and then the George & Dragon Public House; these ancient coaching inns still take guests. I like to look for the lead plaque "fire marks" above some doors, which are testimony to the unchanging self-interest practices of insurance companies. In earlier centuries, only they operated fire wagons, and each company had its own fire mark design so that their wagons would be sure to put out fires for their customers only. I also enjoy spotting historically significant architectural clues like windows that were blocked to avoid the window tax that existed from 1696 to the 1800's, and the widths of chimney bricks—the thinner the bricks, the older the edifice.

By the time I completed my walk, it was only eleven o'clock, which was a bit early to drop in on Silvia, so I meandered over to the post office, which in English villages occupies a corner of the local grocery store whose owner usually deals in stamps, sausages, and gossip. I like to browse in such emporiums because it's a great place to pick up on what's happening in the village. There were notices on the bulletin board of upcoming events and items for sale. "Archery lessons with White Leaf Bowmen

at their ground adjacent to the Rose & Crown."
Right below was, "For sale, IBMXT hard disk drive,
Epson LX800 printer." I guess the fifteenth and
twentieth centuries can comfortably coexist.

In a place so small and inbred, the Spanish lady
at 21 Crown Court must get more than her share
of notice.

"Good morning," I said to the gray-haired
woman in a pink woolen jumper set, who looked
out from behind the post office cage. "Where could
I buy a map of the village?"

I already had three, but it pleases storekeepers
when you buy something, especially when it's
something that shows interest in their hometown,
which is why I have a drawerful of maps; they're
the perfect double duty purchase when you want
a little information.

After paying for the map, I told her I was a
writer who wanted to use this charming village as
a locale, and that I was also here to visit an ac-
quaintance. She was delighted about the author
bit—people like to feel they're contributing to
creativity—and she immediately advised me to
visit West Wycombe Park, the famous stately home
of the Dashwood family which is at the edge of the
village. I didn't tell her I had been there many
times, not as a paying visitor but as a guest of the
current resident, the present Sir Francis, the elev-
enth baronet, and it was a hoot. The original Sir
Francis, the second baronet, had the combination
of wild eccentricity and enormous wealth which
causes some millionaires like Howard Hughes to
end up with six-inch fingernails in a sanitized
locked room, but in Sir Francis' case resulted in a

heritage of beautiful but bizarre creations. Born in
1708, he had a father who had the consideration to
die when Francis was young enough to enjoy in-
heriting the title and the substantial fortune that
went with it. At the age of sixteen, he embarked on
a trip that took him through France, Italy, Ger-
many, Greece, Russia, and Asia Minor, came home
to be caught up in the then current rage for classical
revival, and set about remodeling the rather staid
Queen Anne family home to conform to his new
enthusiasm. A man of fierce individuality and
somewhat peculiar sense of humor, he did not turn
over control to a fashionable architect as others did
but engaged draftsmen who were instructed to ex-
ecute his ideas and fantasies. Over succeeding
years, he continued to remodel and restyle and re-
construct as the whim took him. There are stone
busts of Greek gods, an entrance hall like a Roman
atrium, a Temple of Venus featuring some exam-
ples of Sir Francis' tongue-in-cheek eroticism, Tus-
can and Corinthian columns, and many follies,
those useless but charming little structures that began to dot the English landscape in the eighteenth
century. He dammed the stream and created a lake
in the form of a swan, and built a Temple of Music
on an island in the middle. It's a charming place to
visit, with little footpaths that allow you to wander
through stands of trees and small bridges and offer
the fun of coming upon surprises.

When she finished regaling me with the features
of the Park, she asked me who I was visiting. English villagers tend to clam up when outsiders ask
about local folk. But I figured in no way would
Silvia qualify as a local. In some villages, even if

your ancestors fought alongside Richard the Lion Heart, it takes three generations of residency in the town before you can be considered a native. So what chance would a real foreigner have? Sometimes people with special warmth and charm can win a sort of minimum-level acceptance from the old-time villagers, but Silvia's less-than-sparkling personality precluded that possibility. When I told the postmistress whom I was visiting, her face took on that tight look of stern disapproval that I used to get from Miss Tabey, my third grade teacher, when she asked me if I would like to put away all the erasers and I said No. You'd think she would eventually learn how to frame the question a little more positively, but she never learned. Neither did I. The postmistress' pursed lips indicated that henceforth nothing would issue forth from them, but fortunately for me, curiosity won out. Apparently Silvia kept strictly to herself, the townsfolk knew very little about her, and the post lady felt that her own lack of knowledge of this interloper threatened her status as The Gossip Distribution Center for the town. All anyone knew was that Silvia was the head of the biggest company in High Wycombe.

"She has a Spanish name, but she's not very dark," she said.

"Some Spanish are dark-skinned, but not all. Matter of fact, their king, Don Juan de Carlos, is a blue-eyed blond."

"But all those friends of hers with those black eyes and black hair. The men—and there are plenty of those," she said meaningfully, "all seem to have black beards and mustaches. Some of them are rather frightening-looking," she added. I heard the echo in my head of Luis' words, *"Silvia's interest in Islam is social."*

"Perhaps they're not Spanish," I said.

"Well, one of them isn't, I know that for sure. That Anwar is in and out of there all the time."

"Who's Anwar?"

"He's the boy Sir Francis brought back with him from the Middle East last year." With the usual British reverence, she lowered her voice two decibels when pronouncing the name of aristocracy.

"Is he a boyfriend?" I asked.

She looked shocked. "My dear! He's at least fifteen years younger than she is."

Out of the question, of course. What would any thirtyish woman want with a seventeen-year-old who's at the peak of his sexual powers?

She told me that Anwar was sort of a handyman around town and worked at the church and the old Pilgrims' Rest House.

I thanked her for her invaluable guidance and headed for Silvia's. It was almost noon and I figured we could have lunch in one of the inns. I know that gourmets pale at the prospect of eating English village fare, but I must confess a fondness for gravy-covered mutton, marrows, and steamed cabbage. I walked into the Unicorn Inn to make a reservation. You're probably wondering why I would think I had to book a table for midweek lunch at a restaurant in a town where I hadn't seen more than three people on the street in the last half hour, but I know these small establishments have limited seating capacity and often do meals so reasonably that many of the local elderly pensioners take lunch there regularly. Two white-haired men in their seventies with weather-beaten complexions sat at the bar, each with a large dog sleeping at his feet. They looked at me with total disinterest and then went back to staring into their beers. The woman behind the bar had curled home-hennaed red hair which sat ludicrously atop her heavily wrinkled face and looked like the reverse of a little girl dressed up in her mother's clothes.

"May I book a table for two for lunch?" I asked her, "and could you kindly tell me what's on the menu today?"

"Having beef-and-kidney pie," she said.

Then I heard another voice saying sharply, "No, Mum, that was yesterday," and a sturdy blond woman of about forty bustled in, obviously the patroness. "She gets her days a bit muddled, does Mum," she said. "We're full up at twelve. Could maybe fit you in half after, and today I'm doing lamb stew," she said brusquely in a take-it-or-leave-it tone as she started to rinse out glasses. Ah, another of that charmless English breed of publican who regards her hostelry as strictly business. I supply food and drink; if you're looking for gracious hospitality, mate, try the Savoy. If she's booked solid, either her cooking is better than her personality or her prices are fantastically cheap. Somehow I suspected the second. I arranged for a table for two at twelve-thirty and headed for Silvia's.

Crown Court is a group of cottages reached by passing under an arch on the High Street. Unlike the houses on the main street which are bang on the thoroughfare and have passersby peering in their windows, residents of Crown Court enjoy some privacy as well as gardens and even garages. Although most of the homes were attached row houses, number 21 had the luxury of standing alone. I didn't see the decorators' van in the court-yard, so I guessed they were either finished or had not yet arrived. I rang the bell. After a few minutes, I rang again. Perhaps it wasn't working so I knocked. Then finally, I tried the door and it was open. Unlocked doors in London or New York were no-no's, but were quite conceivable in a small neighborly hamlet. I walked into a small foyer with a gold-framed mirror over an inlaid table bearing a silver salver for visitors' cards of the kind that was the old-time prerequisite in upper-class homes where "paying calls" upon friends was a daily pas-time. I thought Silvia was being slightly over-optimistic. At the moment, a solitary card rested on the tray. Of course, I picked it up and read it. It said, "Desmond Decorators," and had a note on the back: "Will be back Monday at 13:00." Today was Friday. I walked into the lounge, which is Brit-ish for living room—no one there. I tried the kitchen, which had obviously been recently mod-ernized at great expense. It had that German design where all the appliances are camouflaged behind identical wood-paneled fronts and are lined up to present a flush wooden wall. It's very handsome and Teutonically neat, but when I'm hungry or thirsty, I wouldn't like to lose five minutes trying to remember which panel hides the fridge and which the washing machine.

I walked back to the foyer, stood at the foot of the small staircase, and called, "Silvia!" I began to feel a bit disquieted. Perhaps I should go upstairs, but she could have just stepped out for something and might be miffed if she returned to find me prowling around her bedrooms. On the other hand, she could be in the bath. I'm not a patient type, as I've mentioned before, and I don't wait well. So I mounted the staircase calling her name as I went. I came to one bedroom that had the unoccupied look of a guest room. And then I came to what was apparently the master bedroom, which, in this small house, must have come about by breaking down walls and making two rooms into one. There was a large bed with pink linens in a large floral feminine pattern that seemed inappropriate to Silvia's somewhat butchy persona, but I guessed everyone must have some illusions. The bed was unmade and rumpled. On both sides. I turned and saw myself reflected in a huge mirrored dressing table. But there was another woman sitting in front of me. She was slumped over a pink silk brocade bench with her head resting on the table. I stood for a moment and then walked over, bent down and peered into her face, being careful not to touch her or anything else. It was Silvia. Her face and neck were dark red, and there was a straight line purplish bruise around her neck. Her hands and feet were blue. She was dead.

I stood there in shock as the tears coursed down my cheeks. I have seen murdered bodies before, but I can never become inured to the utter tragedy of a person being destroyed because of the whim or wildness of another human being. My first reaction is anger at the waste of a life, followed by compassion for the unimaginable last-minute agony of the victim, and then sadness for the surviv-

ing loved ones. Good God, poor Dona Isabella and
Don Roderigo. I avoided the phone in the room
and went downstairs to the lounge and called Luis.
Then I phoned the Unicorn Inn to cancel my lunch
reservation. Am I cool and considerate or what?
After hanging up, I noticed a large beautiful French
desk at the window. Not being a doctor, dentist,
private eye, or house-breaker, I don't carry plastic
gloves. I hesitated for all of three seconds, whipped
off my scarf, and used it to cover my hands as I
went through all the drawers. I looked carefully for
memos, papers, appointment books, but found
nothing. Either she kept everything in her office, or
there's a safe somewhere. I looked around the
walls, which were covered with excellent copies of
paintings I had seen in the Prado and a genuine
Hockney, which seemed out of place among all the
old masters. With my trusty kerchief in my hand,
I moved the Hockney aside. Voilà, a wall safe. Safe-
cracking not being part of my CV, I replaced the
Hockney and called the police.

X

DR. OGILVY LEANED over the body and felt for the pulse in the neck and examined the line around her neck. He did all this very slowly and then looked at Chief Inspector Thornley appraisingly for a few seconds, and I realized the reason for his hesitation. He was trying to figure a way to tell Thornley what to do without damaging his dignity. There were procedures to be followed with which the doctor, who told me he had retired to West Wycombe after spending twenty-five years as a police surgeon in London, was quite familiar but were totally beyond the experience and competence of the local constabulary. Chief Inspector Thornley was a tall, slow-moving man with the jowls and gut of an ale drinker. From his agitated expression, I guessed that he had enjoyed his fifteen years on the force without ever having encountered anything more serious than house break-ins and stolen vehicles.

I was amazed at how quickly they had arrived

after my call, until I remembered that the modern two-story building around the corner at the top of the High Street was the town hall and police station. Dr. Ogilvy, Chief Inspector Thornley, and Detective Sergeant Parnell rang the bell ten minutes after I had asked the operator for the police. I took them upstairs immediately, and while the doctor conducted his examination of the body, Inspector Thornley conducted his examination of me, while the pop-eyed-with-excitement young sergeant took notes. Thornley was the kind of heavy-footed plodder who tried to substitute bluster for brains. From the banality of his questions, I knew this must be his first murder case. And from the hostility in his attitude, I realized he figured he had the alleged perpetrator.

"You might want to call Chief Constable Stobbart in High Wycombe, Bert," said the doctor. "If I remember, Miss Lopez was the head of the biggest software company in the city. I think he'll want to be in on this."

Thornley cleared his throat and shifted his feet, the classic activity of a balker. I could see he was agonizing over how to evaluate the case's possible effect on his future. It could be the opportunity of a lifetime that could catapult him into an exalted position like Deputy Superintendent of Buckinghamshire C.I.D. On the other hand, he could make a total balls-up that would go down on his record and prevent any further progress in his career.

As long as we were trying to hit our Bert with a dose of reality, I thought I'd add my little bomb.

"Actually, her name is not Silvia Lopez."

Thornley's eyes lit up. A clue. "You mean that's an alias?"

"Not exactly," I said. "Her full name is Dona Silvia Lopez de Lerma Avila. She's the daughter of the Marqués de Mantua, Don Roderigo Lopez de Lerma, the king of Spain's special emissary to the Belgian royal court."

Thornley's face registered a battle between dismay and relief. He was off the hook. The fantasy was finished, but he no longer had to subject his minimal intelligence to the torture of making a decision.

"It'll be out of your hands, Bert," Dr. Ogilvy said with obvious satisfaction. "She's a royal. This will probably involve the Home Secretary, I wouldn't be surprised. They'll want to bring the Yard in for sure."

The young sergeant almost bounced with excitement. "You mean we'll be working with Scotland Yard, sir?"

"Don't get over the moon, laddie," the inspector said glumly. "All it means is we'll have to do all the dog work and they'll get all the credit."

I felt myself get hot with anger. "A young woman is lying here dead, brutally murdered . . . two parents will suffer grief forever—and you two are concerned with career opportunities?"

The inspector turned brick red. Then we heard a car. He looked out of the window which faced the courtyard. When he turned back to us, he seemed stunned.

"It's him—Detective Chief Superintendent Franklin."

Even I had heard of Caleb Franklin—he was

Scotland Yard's star murder expert of the moment. He seemed to have the kind of charisma that catches the fancy of the media. Maybe because he had achieved an almost perfect record of successful solutions of some high-profile murders. Or perhaps because he was a Cambridge-educated black man who had risen to the top of a police force that was reputedly unfriendly to people of color and resentful of the elitely educated. I suspected that Don Roderigo had immediately phoned the Home Secretary to make sure the case got top level treatment. I later learned that the reason Franklin got here so soon was that they were able to reach him at his hotel in Oxford where he was working on the case of a British businessman who had been kidnapped and held for ransom in Iran.

We heard the front door open, and Thornley called down, "Up here, sir."

He literally burst into the room, followed by a tall, thin young man who seemed to be out of breath just following this large, tan-skinned dynamo. I was prepared to dislike Franklin, because I have found that most stars, heroes, and politicians are concerned only with themselves and those who can help them. But you had to like this man immediately; he was extremely attractive and exuded a warmth and energy that was contagious. He wore a beautifully tailored gray tweed jacket, gray flannel trousers, and a sparkling white oxford shirt with a red rep tie. He carried them casually as though he cared about appearance but was not obsessed with clothes. A button on his left sleeve was hanging, which I later learned was endemic to all his jackets as he invariably caught his sleeves on rushed-through doorways.

"Max!" he shouted with pleasure as he walked over with hand outstretched to Dr. Ogilvy. "I heard you had disappeared into the hills somewhere. We miss you."

The doctor beamed. "It's good to see you, Caleb," he said. "Though I must say I don't miss you. I have a nice peaceful practice, and in the ten years I've been doing police work here, this is my first murder, as I think it may be for Inspector Thornley."

The inspector stepped forward. "Chief Inspector Bert Thornley in charge of the West Wycombe station, sir. This is my Detective Sergeant Parnell."

I'm always amazed at how the British react to an upper-class voice. The instant they hear that public school diction, you expect them to tug at their forelocks. The inspector and his sergeant were prepared to be respectful to the superintendent's rank, but it was the accent that awed them.

Franklin nodded. "I'd appreciate if you'd help us set up a Murder Room Report Centre somewhere, Inspector. Sergeant Jarvis here will be glad to help."

"Yes, sir," said Thornley. "We have a nice big back room at the station that I think would be grand. And Mrs. Dunley's tea shop right across the way does lovely seedcakes and buns."

Franklin smiled slightly as he recognized where the inspector placed his priorities. Working on homicides demands long hours and an enforced diet of local take-out foods which usually run to the unrecognizable and indigestible. I often wonder if some murders aren't solved faster because the police ran out of Rennies and Alka-Seltzer and they literally couldn't stomach the work any longer.

He walked over to the body.

"Well, Max, what do we have?"

"Strangulation, and I'd say a neat job by someone who knows how to use a garrote. No other bruises, no sign of any proverbial heavy instrument. I'll know more after I do the autopsy, of course. As for sexual activity prior to death, all you have to do is examine the bedclothes—the odor and evidence of semen is quite evident."

Inspector Thornley cleared his throat loudly and looked over at me. How sweet, I thought, he's embarrassed. I tried to remember the last time a man tried to shield me from prurient language, and I thought it was in third grade when Carl Tanner punched Barry Birnbaum because he said "smelly tinky doo" in front of me.

Suddenly Superintendent Franklin noticed me. "And who is this?" he asked.

"It's the lady who found the body, sir," said Thornley. "A Ms. Emma Rhodes," with a heavy accent on the "Ms."

The superintendent's face was totally impassive, which I found surprising. It's not that I expect all men to start slathering at the mouth with desire when they meet me for the first time, but I usually get some sign of approval. However, since policemen should scrupulously avoid any emotional reaction to persons involved in a crime, I regarded his blank expression as strictly professional. Suddenly his face changed from bland to quizzical.

"Wait a minute—I know you from somewhere."

He kept staring. "I didn't actually meet you ... I would certainly remember that."

Aha—a touch of the personal slips in. He shook his head as though to roust the memory from among the little gray cells. "Faces are my business—I never forget ... I know!" he shouted triumphantly. "You're the woman who blocked the Belgian kidnapping of the queen's nephew!" He looked at me with new interest.

Inspector Thornley stared at me with amazement, and I believe I lost my standing as his prime suspect at that moment. "That's right. We saw you on the telly. Fancy that. Wait till I tell the missus."

My heroine status had an effect on all the constabulary. The superintendent instructed Sergeant Jarvis to take me downstairs and put me in a nice comfortable chair in the lounge. Then he turned to me with a smile that lit up the room.

"Would you mind terribly waiting? I'll be down in a few minutes. I'd like to speak to you."

When the superintendent finally came into the lounge fifteen minutes later, he was apologetic for the delay. He was ever so polite and respectful, but I'd been questioned by enough police to know that this was frequently a tactic that preceded the rubber hose.

He sat down in a facing chair and looked at me with a disarming smile. "Well, Miss Rhodes, you seem to have a rare talent for being where things are happening. The question is, are you the catalyst, or just an unwitting bystander? And are the events related?"

"Superintendent—I could never be an unwitting anything. And yes, the events are linked only because of the people involved. Silvia's family is related to Queen Fabiola, which is indirectly how we met.''

I heard heavy footsteps coming down the stairs and looked to see them carrying the bagged body. I shivered slightly and he showed immediate concern.

''Is it chilly in here? I'll ask my sergeant to light a fire.''

I shook my head. ''It's not the temperature, it's the circumstances.''

Murder is such a violation of privacy . . . all the victim's most personal belongings become just things, her whole carefully constructed environment gets torn apart, the nakedness of her life and her body become totally exposed. The violence of the murder is cruel enough; the aftermath violence committed upon her seems de trop.

A steady stream of men tramped up and down the stairs carrying lights, cables, cameras, and all sorts of equipment needed at the scene of a murder. The body and the room had to be photographed from all angles. The fingerprint expert had to do his work, and a team would go through everything, drawer by drawer.

''Murder is the ultimate violation of a person because it destroys life,'' said the superintendent. ''It's the grossest of indignities that can be inflicted upon a human being, and it's the policeman's duty to punish the perpetrator. But we never forget that what's now a corpse was once a person and what may seem disrespectful is merely what must be done in the pursuit of justice.''

The thinking man's cop. His very expressive

dark brown eyes registered a deep and intelligent intensity. No wonder this guy is such a success. He's either a very fine human being or a terrific actor. Or maybe both.

"Did you know Ms. Lopez well?" he asked.

"We met once in her parents' home in Bruges," I said. "Look, I know that the person who finds the body is considered an immediate suspect—especially since Silvia was undoubtedly killed by someone she knew. However, I did not kill her, and if you check with the postmistress, you'll find she and I were deep in conversation when the murder took place."

"How do you know she was killed by someone she knew, and how do you know when she died?" he asked softly.

I sat back and looked directly at him. "Since she was looking in the mirror when she was garroted, she must've seen the murderer and trusted him completely to allow him to come that close. There was no sign of the kind of struggle that would have occurred had she seen a stranger approach. Her face and neck are red from strangulation, but the rest of her skin is waxy and her hands and feet are blue which means she has been dead for over thirty minutes."

"Of course, I forgot that you are a writer," he said. That's how the Brussels' headlines described me. "May I assume you write murder mysteries?"

I let my silence allow him to draw whatever inference he desired. It's so much easier that way. I really hate out-and-out lying.

" 'Scuse me, Gov." His sergeant came into the

room. "Can we search this room? We've done a first go-over in the others."

I watched as the sergeant worked with Sergeant Parnell. They wore gloves and carefully examined all drawers. I got up as though I were restless and began to walk around the room.

"Oops!" I tripped slightly on the rug in front of the Hockney and fell against it, moving it askew. They saw the safe immediately.

"Let's get that opened. Call the Yard and ask them to send out someone from the safe squad," said Franklin.

"You don't have to bother Metro," said a voice from the door. It was Dr. Ogilvy. "You see, I'm not the only retiree from the criminal world here. Picker Shaftoe is spending his golden years in High Wycombe. He has a little smoke shop on the High Street."

The superintendent laughed. "The Picker lives here? As I remember, there wasn't a lock he couldn't pick or a safe he couldn't open. I hope the county men are keeping an eye on him."

"Indeed we are, sir," said Thornley, who appeared behind the doctor. He cleared his throat. "Matter of fact, he sometimes helps us out when the need arises."

Franklin raised his eyebrows. "Mr. Moreland, manager of the Midland Bank, locked himself in the vault a while back and it was our Picker who got him home for dinner," said Dr. Ogilvy.

One hour later, a beaming Picker swung open the door of Silvia's safe. "Ain't lost me touch, have I?" he said proudly. "But don't none of you coppers worry, my missus would have a right fit if I went back to the old ways. She's a grand girl, but you've seen nowt yet till you've seen my Jennie in a temper."

My writer status entitled me to a front seat as the contents of the safe were spread out on the table. There was some jewelry and a brown leather box. When the box was opened, there were gasps in the room. Five packages of what were later counted to be 200,000 pounds each lay before us. There was also a card with a list of five phone numbers and dates, which I memorized. I did mention that I had a photographic memory, didn't I?

"That's a lot of pin money to keep around the house, even for a wealthy woman," said Franklin. "Get it bagged and marked, Sergeant." He slipped the card in his pocket. "Is there any place to get a bite and a beer around here, Inspector?"

Thornley mentioned the three inns plus the tea shop.

"Miss Rhodes and I are going to the Swan Inn— you men take your pick of the others." He turned to me. "That is, if you don't mind breaking bread with a copper."

There were many curious glances cast our way as we sat at our table. The news of the murder was all around the town by now, of course, and Franklin had already twice politely but firmly put off the reporter from the *High Wycombe Times*, who was obviously dreaming of the scoop of a lifetime that would give him the ticket to feature-writing fame in a major city newspaper.

"He's a pest," I said.

Franklin shrugged. "He has a job to do just as I. Besides, I've always found it wise to work with the press. They can be quite helpful by spreading information we need publicized, and sometimes even cooperate to the point of holding back on details that require discretion."

I ordered salad and cider and he did, too, which didn't surprise me. He was a large man but with a trim and 99% fat-free physique that indicated hours spent at the gym. When I commented on his excellent eating habits, he told me he was a vegetarian.

"I've always disliked the idea that an animal has to be killed for my pleasure. I have no problem filling my belly satisfactorily without destroying a life to do it."

"Was this abhorrence for killing the reason you became a homicide detective?" I asked.

He seemed thunderstruck for a moment. "Actually, I never connected the two—but now that I think about it, you're probably right. The finality of an inflicted death is unconscionable to me."

"Does that mean you're against capital punishment?" I asked.

"Yes."

I sat back in my chair and regarded him with a smile. "You're a strange combination for a policeman. An anti-capital-punishment Cambridge graduate who's a vegetarian."

"And is black," he finished.

"You are? I thought you'd just come back from two weeks in Tenerife. With those credentials, what on earth made you join the police? Or is another one of your qualifications that you're a card-carrying masochist?"

"Believe me, there are days when I wonder. My

father taught me that punishment is necessary to maintain a civilized society, but that it must be administered in a civilized way if we are to survive as a civilized society. I wanted to be sure it was."

"Your father sounds like an unusual person."

"He is, as is my mother. They're both schoolteachers."

You know how I like men who like their parents. He told me that his ancestor was an American slave, Caleb Franklin, who had come to England with Benjamin Franklin, who taught him to read and write and then freed him. Caleb married an English schoolteacher, settled down, and raised a family of seven children, all of whom became schoolteachers, a profession that remained in the family for generations. The current Caleb was the first to have left the field of education.

"How did you come to deal solely in murder?"

He smiled. "I don't. I've just been involved in a kidnapping."

"Oh, the British businessman who's being held by Iranian terrorists. I read about that in the *Times* yesterday."

"Yes, it's yesterday's news, all right," he said wryly. "He's been returned home safely."

"Another Caleb Franklin success?"

He grimaced. "Hardly. Another Naji success, I'm afraid."

"Who or what is a Naji?"

"It's Farsi for 'The Savior.' He's some mystery man who's made it his cause to rescue businessmen kidnapped in Iran."

"Maybe it's the Iranian government's way to get financing to build nuclear reactors, since they can't seem to get what they want from the United States Congress—but then, who can?"

"The ransom notes are signed by some sect whose name escapes me. So far this Naji has rescued five. He seems to have access to people and places we don't, and of course," he said bitterly, "he's not handicapped by having to observe diplomatic delicacy."

I was intrigued. "They seek him in heaven, they seek him in hell, that damned elusive Pimpernel."

He was not amused. "You think it's funny. The newspapers print the story of the kidnapping one day, this Naji contacts the victim's company the next day and offers to get their man freed, and by the time we get our official machinery going, he has the man home and we look like a bunch of inept bumblers."

"Does the Naji get paid for these services?" I asked.

"The company pays him ten percent of the unpaid ransom."

"And what's the usual ransom figure?"

"Two million pounds."

That meant his fee came to 200,000 pounds. And I thought I was in a good business. But then, he has to deal with terrorists who probably reek of unwashed bodies and indigestible foods while I get to hang out with a nicer class of people. After all money isn't everything. Well, not quite.

"Emma, *querida*. They told me you were here. I'm so glad to have found you."

Luis stood at our table. I jumped up and hugged him.

"Luis—I'm so sorry." I turned to Franklin and introduced them.

Franklin stood up to extend his condolences and asked Luis to join us. I could see him looking from Luis to me speculatively to assess our relationship.

I was puzzled. "Luis, how did you get here so soon? Wasn't I speaking to you less than an hour ago in Brussels?"

He looked distracted. "No, when you call my phone number it reaches me wherever I am. I took the 7:31 a.m. tunnel train this morning. I've been in our offices in High Wycombe." His expression darkened and he turned to Caleb.

"Did Emma tell you that most of my sister's friends were Islamic?" said Luis. "They are a rather savage people and killing comes easily to them. I'm afraid I never got to know any of them so that I don't know—yet—who was her current lover. But when I do . . ." His face was tight with fury.

"We will find him, Don Luis," Franklin said. "And we will find and punish," he said pointedly, "the person who killed your sister."

Luis looked surprised. "Surely you believe they are one and the same man?"

"At this point, I don't allow myself to believe anything. I've always found it best to keep my mind as open as possible and let painstaking police work lead me. A detective avoids jumping to early conclusions for fear it will prevent him from looking further and perhaps finding the truth. My men are doing house-to-house questioning right now and will check out everyone who has been with your sister in the recent past."

Somehow I don't imagine that every victim's

next of kin gets this succinct summary of pertinent police activities. The importance of Luis' family has apparently not escaped Franklin, and he's handling the matter with both diplomacy and firmness. I especially like the way he let Luis know that any tactics of familial retribution that might be part of the Spanish culture were unacceptable in England.

A phone went off and both men reached for theirs. It was for Luis, but this time he excused himself and went off somewhere to converse privately. Obviously the presence of Scotland Yard inhibited him.

"I think your friend wishes to be more than a friend," said Caleb (after two ciders, we were on a first name basis).

"I'm not looking for any more-than-friends right now," I said.

"Do I take it your dance card is full?" he asked.

"I merely said I wasn't looking. That doesn't preclude the possibility of an interesting chance encounter."

Luis returned to the table. "That was my father. He wanted to be sure that the famous Detective Superintendent Franklin was working on Silvia's . . . death." He obviously could not get himself to say "murder."

Caleb rose and said, "I'm afraid I have a sad task to ask of you. We need someone to officially identify the body."

"Of course," said Luis.

"One of my men will take you to High Wycombe."

"Yes, I must get back to the office," said Luis. "Silvia ran the company, you know. She is—was—

a fine businesswoman. I don't know how we'll get along without her."

"I'll meet you there," said Caleb. "I'll want to talk to the people who worked with your sister."

Luis turned to me. "Can you come, too, Emma?"

Here I was wondering how I could wangle a tag-along invitation from Caleb without showing anything more than casual interest. The police are very proprietary about their cases and dislike interference even from seasoned colleagues in other districts. If the superintendent had a hint of my professional interest, I'd be spending the rest of the day on a hard bench in the Report Centre.

"I'd be glad to, Luis." Then I turned to Caleb with what I hoped came across as a shy, tentative smile, but since demure is not a natural part of my persona, I had a bit of a problem with the presentation. "If the superintendent doesn't mind." From the amused smirk on Caleb's face, it was apparent he wasn't buying.

"I'd be delighted to have your company, Emma, as long as you don't fancy being Jessica Fletcher and expect to solve the case within sixty minutes."

After Luis left with one of Caleb's constables, I thought it was time to mention Anwar.

"Yes, my men have been told about him," said Caleb. "He seems to have done a bunk and they're hunting for him. We'll turn him up," he said.

Sure, but when? Plodding police routine is fine when you're just working toward your pension, but I operate on a more accelerated timetable. I told him I'd meet him within the hour at the Report Centre and headed down the High Street. I walked to the Pilgrims' Rest House and circled the old building, peering at the roofline. Then I went inside and looked up until I spotted a small door in the corner ceiling. Standing on a chair, I pulled it open and called softly, "Anwar!"

He was just a boy. Crouched on a pile of blankets, he looked at me with such abject fear that I felt like patting him on the head and giving him a cookie and milk.

"Don't be frightened, I'm not the police."

Apparently going *to* the police was an alien concept in his country, where keeping away from all government officials was one of the keys to survival. Law and order in Anwar's hometown was probably handled simply and summarily: torture first and talk later. I managed to assure him that the British police dealt only in solving crimes, not punishing them, and he finally agreed to come with me.

When I walked in with Anwar, Caleb looked up from his desk and smiled. "Miss Fletcher, I presume. And I expect this is Anwar." He arose and said, "You can tell me later how you found him, but now let's get him into an interrogation room."

Anwar moaned piteously and sagged against me.

"You'd better reassure him, Superintendent; in his country, people only leave such rooms feet first."

He sat at a table sipping tea, with Caleb and Sergeant Jarvis sitting opposite. I was allowed to stay because he became almost hysterical when I started to leave. Tears streamed down his face as he talked about Silvia. Apparently she was the only person in the village who saw past the dark skin to recognize an intelligent sensitive young man who was lonely and homesick in a very strange and cold land. He did errands for her, fixed little things in the house, and was a general all-around helper who must have been extremely handy for a single woman living alone.

"Did she pay you?"

"Of course. She told me a man who works must be paid," he said proudly.

I began to think there was a lot more to Silvia than met my perhaps overcritical eye.

"Did she have many visitors?" asked Caleb.

"She was a nice lady—she had many friends."

"Was there one special friend?" he asked casually.

Anwar hesitated. "Yes."

"What did he look like?"

Anwar shook his head. "I never saw him, but I knew when he was to be there." He described how happy and excited Silvia became when he was expected. "I was always sent out to get special things for his meal."

"Did she expect him today?" asked Caleb.

Anwar shook his head. "No, yesterday he was to come."

Caleb got up and signaled Sergeant Jarvis to take over. He walked over to me and said softly, "We don't know if he was Islamic."

Anwar heard. "Oh, no, he was not of Islam," he said firmly.

"If you never saw him, how do you know that?" Sergeant Jarvis asked quickly.

"I had always to go to the store and buy for her

a large ham because it was his favorite meal. It is forbidden for us to eat such meat."

"The sergeant will ask you some more questions, Anwar, and then he will take you home or wherever you wish to go," said Caleb. He spoke especially gently. "But please stay in the village as we may need to talk to you again. Thank you very much for your help."

Anwar's face broke into a broad smile and he looked at me as though he would wash my feet. "Could not I stay with you, Missy Emma? I can take good care of you."

He's looking for a Silvia substitute. I'm not even tempted, although I have to admit I always had a sneaking envy of Sir Peter Wimsey's Bunter. It's nice to have someone else take care of your clothes, your food, and your home and all the nitty-gritty scut work of living. But in order to live successfully with servants, you have to be able to totally ignore their presence so that you feel no sense of infringement of privacy. I've always marveled at the aristocracy's they-don't-count attitude that enables them to say and do whatever they wish in front of the help. I find it difficult to ignore anything or anyone, and I'd probably end up making Anwar chicken soup when he had a cold. Besides, having a schleppalong genie somehow conflicts with my independent image. Which was probably why Caleb had that look of amusement on his face as I explained to the crestfallen young man that I had no need for his services—any of them.

Caleb looked at his watch. "Don Luis must be at the offices now. We'd better get going."

XI

~~~

IT WAS A group of low buildings set in extensive grounds that were landscaped in that perfectly symmetrical sterile style I call Contemporary Industrial Park, with a large sign that said, SATCOM LTD. The security guards at the entry desk directed us to the executive floor where Luis awaited us at the reception desk. We now had two High Wycombe detective sergeants with us whom we had picked up when Caleb made the courtesy call required when stepping into another district's bailiwick.

"What and who would you like to see, Superintendent?" Luis asked.

"Your sister's office first, please."

As we walked into the huge carpeted office, a man was seated at the glass desk working on the computer. He jumped up when he saw us.

"Hugh, what are you doing in Silvia's office?" Luis asked sharply.

"Just looking for some data that Silvia and I were working on, Luis."

If you're working together, I wondered, how come you don't have it in your computer, too? And why do you act like a guy who's been caught dealing cards from the bottom of the deck?

"This is Hugh Eddington, our vice president and general manager," said Luis. Before Luis could continue the introductions, Eddington walked straight toward Caleb with a neon smile.

"Detective Superintendent Franklin, I'm honored to meet you."

I've only known the man three seconds and I already know that he's a osmarmy sleaze. To confirm that conclusion, he gave me the eyeballing flick-over used by politicians and other power-parasites to instantly evaluate whether you're worth talking to. He's the kind of man who constantly looks over your shoulder at parties to be sure no one more important than you has arrived.

"Oh, and this is Emma Rhodes, a good friend," said Luis, smiling at me.

I rate; the guy nearly tripped over the coffee table to reach out for my hand. "Delighted to meet you, Miss Rhodes." He used the Hollywood super-sincere shake: grab the hand with your right and the arm with your left.

"I'd like to talk with you later, Mr. Eddington," said Caleb. "But right now, I want to look over Ms. Lopez's office." You could see that Eddington was dying to stay, but the note of dismissal was unmistakable.

After he left, I said with obvious distaste, "He's a real charmer, that one."

Luis seemed surprised. "Hugh? He's our most skilled software development engineer and an excellent businessman—an unusual combination. Silvia and my father think very highly of him. In fact, they were talking about making him president and Silvia the CEO."

He may be a whiz with computers, I thought, but I wouldn't let him near the books. And what about you, Luis, where do you fit into this equation?

"If you need me, Superintendent, my office is just across the corridor. If I am not in, my secretarial watchdog, Miss Ballard, will know where to reach me." He smiled at the young woman who was sitting at the desk in front of his door. She was breathtaking, one of those pink-cheeked, blue-eyed English beauties who make you wonder if maybe the rainy English climate is good for begetting blooming young women as well as gardens.

He smiled ruefully. "My father gave me an office here hoping I would develop an interest in the business. But Silvia took over things so well, there just didn't seem any reason or place for me."

Caleb walked around Silvia's office as though getting a feel of the place. It's what I do when I want to get a sense of the person who "lived" there. I didn't attempt any overt inspection because I suspected the superintendent would not enjoy seeing me Sherlocking on his case. Actually, I was mainly interested in Silvia's computer and what it contained that was of such interest to Hugh Eddington. No point in bothering to boot it and check it out; if a computer genius like him couldn't find it, then surely I wouldn't. I walked over to the desk and bent over to look at the front drawer.

"Please don't touch anything," Caleb said sharply. "Forensics haven't been here yet."

I clutched my ear and dropped to the floor behind the desk. "Lost an earring," I called out as I
reached into the almost invisible slot I had noticed
under the drawer and pulled out a floppy disk
which I slipped into my handbag.

After Caleb completed his inspection, he instructed the detectives to seal the room, told me he
was going to talk to Hugh Eddington, and suggested I find something to do. Gladly.

As soon as he was out of sight, I went into Luis'
office. He wasn't there, but his computer was. I
popped in the floppy disk, and a list of what
looked like sales records came up on the screen.
There were ten companies located throughout England, France, and Belgium. The data included
quantities of products sold, prices, dates of delivery, and dates of payments. They were apparently
good customers since bills were paid within ten
days, and they reordered steadily every three
months. The records covered almost one year. I
printed and then slipped the floppy and printout
into my bag.

"Emma!" Luis entered the office. "I haven't had
a chance to really talk to you since this dreadful
thing. And you, my *pobrecita*, the horror of finding
Silvia that way." We sat down on the couch in the
corner of the office and I took his hand.

"Never mind me, Luis. How are your parents
taking it?"

He shook his head sadly. "I would have preferred to inform them in person, but unfortunately,
I had to do it by telephone. They were devastated.
But each will handle the grief differently. My
mother, she is the stoic who will cry alone in her

room. My father, like a true grandee, will want to avenge the honor of the family and will be in a constant state of fury which will mask his pain."

"And you, Luis? How do you feel?"

He was thoughtful. "Sadness, anger, and guilt."

"Why guilt?" I asked in surprise.

He leaned back against the cushions and looked straight ahead. "I loved my sister, but I'm afraid I never liked her. You see, I was the favored one—the son, the firstborn, the perfect child who was good at everything. My parents adored me. When she came along, I was, as you Americans say, a hard act to follow. And how she tried, the poor girl. Whatever I did, she emulated and tried to do better. I was a good skier, what they called a natural. Silvia took endless lessons, entered competitions and won medals. I went to Oxford, she followed. I became an Islamic scholar, so of course she had to do the same, but the subject did not suit her type of intelligence. Sadly, she was not the pretty little girl desired by Spanish parents and never got their approval. During our growing-up years, I went to endless parties and balls, but Silvia received few invitations. As you noticed, she defensively developed a rather repellent personality. Psychologists would probably say it's the 'you don't want me so I don't want you' syndrome. But then she found the one area where she alone could star—father's business. She went to the Harvard Business School and became a brilliant businesswoman. Father was very proud of her, but all Mother saw was a daughter who was not married."

"So why should you feel guilty? You did nothing."

He sighed. "Exactly. I did nothing."

The unsaid words "and now it's too late" hung in the silence and I let them. When consoling someone, I'm always mindful that he or she may have painful truths that must be faced, and uttering banal clichés merely trivializes their importance.

After a minute or so, he got up resolutely. "Now I must become involved in the company. It is my responsibility."

"Exactly what do you make here?" I asked.

"We design software systems for computers, and we produce them. My family has had many generations of wealth, mostly in land. When it all came to my father, he decided to diversify and began to buy small companies of many kinds. After Silvia came home from Harvard, she convinced him that putting it all into one large enterprise would lead to greater growth possibilities. When she heard that SATCOM was available, they sold off the other businesses and bought this. And she has managed it superbly. She hired experts like Hugh Eddington and put some top-notch software development engineers on contract. As I believe I told you earlier, the business has quadrupled in five years. But let me show you—I'll give you a tour."

We passed through the quiet area where people sat staring at computer monitors. "This is where the creativity takes place," said Luis. When we came to an area called "Quality Testing," he pointed out that the code must be thoroughly tested before software is released for shipment.

"What's behind those closed doors?" I asked.

"That, my dear, is the R&D department . . . SATCOM's future. We're a leading edge company, and they're constantly doing research and development to keep us that way." He paused and a cloud passed over his face. "It's also the site of Silvia's dream."

"What was that?" I asked.

"She had the concept for a product that would instantly make us one of the major software companies in the world, maybe even equal to Microsoft. It would be a combination hardware and software product that would transmit via Internet image as well as voice. The software would be in the form of a small diskette that would be loaded onto your system. It would include a scanner that would digitize both your voice and live visual image. Think of it—you could see and talk to people anywhere in the world via the Internet instantaneously. Right now, only top level secret government agencies like the CIA and Pentagon have such a system. Silvia's product would make it accessible to everyone."

"It sounds fantastic . . . a personal transmission system. What's happening to it?"

"Sadly, nothing. It requires millions to fully develop, and we don't have that kind of money."

"Why couldn't you raise it—go public?"

"People no longer go public on a dream. Silvia went to some of the biggest companies in the country who are our customers to ask for financing— but none would invest in us. They said they felt we did not have the expertise to develop such a sophisticated product. Silvia was obsessed with developing her idea. I think she had visions of becoming Steve Jobs and Bill Gates all rolled into one." He shook his head. "She was so determined to get the financing—and now . . . she died without realizing her dream."

"Few of us get to realize our dreams, Luis."

We walked through corridors into the next building. "And this is where the manufacturing takes place." Then on to another building which housed the packing and shipping facilities. Software disks were being slipped into small envelopes and put into cartons.

"What are all those big boxes over there?" I asked.

"That's OSS—operational systems software."

"Oh, you mean like Windows. The big ticket items."

"They're packaging Graphics Cards over there. We sell those for one thousand pounds."

All the workers smiled at Luis. You could see he was well liked, but there was deference, too. When I commented on that, Luis frowned. "This is a new attitude, and I don't know if I like it. It seems unfriendly."

"You're the boss man now, Luis—you can't expect them to treat you like a buddy anymore." I noticed the young women stealing tentative glances at Luis. "And I expect your harem of lovelies here will become a little more restrained now that you're Management."

He looked surprised, and then chagrined. "More's the pity. I guess you're right."

I laughed. "Ah, the burdens of responsibility. You'll have to draw up new guidelines of dealing with personnel. You know, friendly but not familiar. The way the women look at you, Luis, I think you may have a lot of retraining ahead."

I watched how each diskette was shrink-wrapped with its accompanying documentation manuals, then put together with the hardware card plus brackets and tools to fit it onto the hard drive, and all put into a large box that was shock-protected with various packaging materials.

A man approached Luis. "Sir, there's a call for you."

He came back to announce that the detective superintendent was ready to leave and awaited us in Luis' office.

"I didn't plan to return to West Wycombe right now, Superintendent," I told Caleb. "I have to get back to Brussels tonight. You can reach me there at the phone number I gave you. You have my full statement," I went on. "I'll come back for the coroner's inquest, of course."

"Are you taking the tunnel train back, Emma?" asked Luis. "I am planning to take the 3:31. It would be nice if we could make the trip together."

"I'd like that, Luis," I said.

"Good! Let me wind up things—I'll meet you right here within a half hour."

After Luis and Caleb and his entourage left, I walked across the hall to Silvia's office and cast one of my guaranteed man-melting smiles upon the constable who was guarding the door. I had pulled off one of my earrings just before.

"I think I dropped an earring in there. Could I just pop in and get it? I won't be a minute."

If I hadn't mentioned it before, I always keep a pair of clip-on earrings in my bag when on a case. You'd be amazed how often I get to use the old "I dropped an earring" gambit.

He was a very young ginger-haired man who was torn between doing his assigned duty conscientiously and the political consequences of mistreating a friend of the big "Guv" from Scotland Yard. He wavered so I brought in the heavy artillery and bent down to adjust my shoe, thereby displaying a generous flash of cleavage.

"All right, Miss—but just for a minute."

I slipped the floppy disk back into Silvia's hiding place, put on my earring, and left. I try to avoid doing anything illegal. Borrowing evidence may be offensive, but it's not a criminal offense.

Luis and I took the train from High Wycombe to London, and there boarded the bullet train. We settled into our comfortable reserved seats for the three-and-a-quarter-hour trip that would take us to the Midi station in Brussels. We chatted for a few minutes, then he got up and said, "Emma, will you excuse me for a moment? I must use the lavatory."

"Better give me your ticket then, Luis, in case the conductor comes through. I can have it punched for you."

I put his ticket together with mine and then idly glanced at it. It looked exactly like mine, of course—but his outgoing date showed Thursday. Mine was today, Friday. He said he came to England today—but he had actually arrived yesterday. Oh, Tyrone, what have you been up to?

My method of solving any problem is to accumulate all pertinent data inside a portion of my head that I call my "Brain Bank," where it sits until I'm ready to deal with it. There's no sense in trying to evaluate the effect of each piece of information as it comes along; it's time-wasting and fruitless because you do not yet have all the facts. Luis' lie and its significance was deposited in the "Brain Bank" to be examined when I have the whole picture.

XII

WHEN I WALKED in the house, I found Esther in the kitchen, slicing onions again. Two shining, freshly baked twisted loaves of challah were on the counter.

"If the Jews have discovered that onions have the penicillin-power of chicken soup, I think it's time they shared their secret with the world."

She looked up and smiled. "My grandmother who was a wonderful cook used to say, 'First you start with an onion.'"

"What are you making?" I asked, sniffing appreciatively. "It smells marvelous."

"It's Friday. I'm making our traditional Shabbat meal: chopped liver, matzo balls in chicken soup, roast chicken, and honey cake. You're welcome to join us. Martin will be back from his trip before sundown."

"Thanks. I'd love to. My mouth is watering already."

She tossed the onions into sizzling fat and began

moving them around in the pan. Without looking up, she said, "So you had an interesting time in England."

It wasn't a question, it was a statement.

"I assume you're using the word 'interesting' as in the Chinese curse, 'May you live in interesting times.' I guess you can consider one aborted assassination and one murder not quite your usual day. I imagine I'll be hearing from Abba. He must be a bit upset with me."

Esther made a face. "Just a bit."

"I know it was risky, but I had to go."

"Would you like to learn how to make chopped liver?" she asked.

The abrupt change of subject conveyed the clear message: "Your business is none of my business." Her job was to save my life but not get involved in it. At the moment, my job is to make a decision: do I really want to know how to make chopped liver?

I admire Spenser's talent with a sauté pan, but I'm usually too busy or tired to fiddle with a griddle, which means my eating usually consists either of going out or bringing in. However, one never knows. Someday I might get stranded on the Gaza Strip with an Israeli lover. It never hurts to develop Jewish survival tactics.

Actually, I found the process fascinating. I watched her throw a batch of cut up raw chicken livers into the pan to cook along with the onions.

"Is that olive oil you're frying with?" I asked.

She shook her head. "Chicken fat—schmaltz. That's the secret." I inhaled deeply and sighed contentedly.

"I know Jews don't proselytize for converts—but

I think if you released that aroma on a crowd, you'd do better than the Pope."

She took the pan off the stove, added three sliced hard-boiled eggs, and transferred the entire mixture to a wooden bowl. Cholesterol City—but what a way to go. She sat in a chair, placed the bowl in her lap, and began chopping with a steady one-two-three beat, adding salt and pepper as she went along, until the mixture had a slightly coarse texture. She put a little bit on a fork and handed it to me.

It didn't seem possible that the taste would be equal to the delicious aroma—but it was. Now I was becoming interested in technique. "How come you don't use your food processor?"

"Hand-chopping preserves the individuality and taste of each ingredient. It also creates a more substantial rough texture, which I prefer. The processor turns it into a smooth pâté."

I looked at her pleadingly with my empty fork. She smiled and placed a small pile on a plate with some crackers, giving me the usual motherly admonishment: "Now don't spoil your appetite for dinner."

She walked over to the stove and pulled out a roasting chicken, which she basted and returned to the oven. Now I wanted to know everything.

"What's that stuff you poured on the chicken?"

"It's a marinade. I put one onion and a half glass of orange juice in the processor and make a sort of paste that I smear all over the chicken and then sprinkle it with a seasoned salt."

"She's too modest to tell you it's her own recipe," said a voice at the door.

"Martin!" Esther's face lit up as he came over to give her a big hug and kiss. He turned to me with his arm still around her. "You're a writer," he said. "If you want to write a book about creative Jewish cooking which you can subtitle 'How to Keep Kosher Without Heartburn'—spend a day in my wife's kitchen."

She looked at him with loving concern. "You look weary, darling. Did you travel a long way today? Was it that customer in England again, the one who seems to give you so much trouble?"

"I never discuss my customer's business or my business publicly, Esther," he said sharply. "That's confidential information. You should know better than that."

But rebuking your wife publicly, that's O.K. A simple "yes" or "no" would have been sufficient. Why do men have the need to establish their authority? That's the kind of stuff that keeps me single.

She looked chastened. "I'm sorry, dear—are you hungry? Would you like some chopped liver?"

The reproving look was replaced by a broad smile and he hugged her again. "My Yiddishe mama—no, darling, I'll wait for dinner. Right now all I want is a hot bath." He looked at my plate of chopped liver. "You'd better watch it, Emma. That stuff is addictive."

I went up to my room to wash up and change, and the phone was ringing as I came in. It was Abba. He was not happy.

"So, Nancy Drew—you maybe thought I was overreacting when I told you they were out to get you? And going off to an apartment that has a se-

curity setup I would only wish on Hitler? A terrace
that could be accessed easily even by a two-
hundred-pound woman with a heart condition?
Are you out of your fucking mind?"

I was contrite because he was right. "But how
did they find me? Except for that note I left for
Esther, I didn't tell anyone I was going to London."

"Even schmucks like the Partisans of God know
some of the basic rudiments of surveillance—like
finding out where the subject has residences. They
probably had a man staking out your London flat,
and there's probably another in Portugal, and another prick in New York."

"Was your man watching my London place?"

"My man was on you from the minute you got
on the train."

I was astounded. "But I looked around me very
carefully all the time. There was no one who looked
Israeli or Iranian or even, as the English call them,
foreign. I remember noting that my train seemed
to be filled with archetypal Brit businessmen."

He snorted. "You goyim. You think all Jews look
Jewish. If you're looking for big noses, check out
the Royal Family. If Princess Anne lived on West
End Avenue in New York, her mother would've
hauled her in for a nose job long ago. A little chin
work wouldn't hurt, either. And Prince Charles
with that huge conk. If I had a nose like that, you'd
say I looked Jewish. But on him, they call it 'aristocratic.' If a goy has a nose like a macaw, it's aq-
uiline. On us—it's Jewish."

"I admit, Abba, that we Wasps have to learn to
kick the stereotype images we have of Jews, just as
you guys have to get over classifying all of us as

pallid, unfeeling zombies who live on white bread and martinis."

I heard a loud guffaw. "All right, you wiseass shiksa, we'll call it a draw. But you gotta stop running around. The Israeli government is not your private protection agency—we can't afford to follow you around."

"Even if I turn up some secret Islamic activities?"

"That murdered woman has some connection?" he asked quickly.

"You know about Silvia's murder?" I asked in surprise.

"I said we had a man on you at the train. You think he dropped you when you got to High Wycombe? He didn't hang around the village too long once he saw you got tied up with Scotland Yard. He figured you were safe enough when you were with Franklin."

"You know of Caleb Franklin?"

He sighed at my ignorance. "If you were Donald Trump, wouldn't you know Ruppert Murdoch? When you're in a business, you have to know the heavy hitters in your line all over the world. Franklin is a star. I never met the man, but I hear he's a hunk. So tell me, did you fuck?"

"Abba, you're too young to be a dirty old man. In answer to your first question, yes—Silvia did have some involvement with terrorists, but I'm not sure of all the details yet. I'll let you know as I know."

"O.K., Ahuvati sweetheart—but try not to get killed before I get all the information."

Time to check in with my favorite Belgian cop.

"Emma! You're back from England and didn't

call me. I was worried—but you're O.K.?"

"Albert, I'm a big girl—I can take care of myself." With a little help from the Mossad, of course.

I made a date with Albert for the following evening. I had a bath and a lie-down during which time I cleared my head of all thoughts; it's the only way to really rest, lying prone won't do the job if your brain keeps churning. Then I went down for dinner.

The dining room table was covered with a snowy white cloth. There were gleaming brass candlesticks at the foot of the table and a covered challah at the other end. There were lovely silver settings and gold-bordered white china dishes and crystal goblets, and a bottle of wine in a silver coaster. It was the first time I had ever seen Esther in a dress, and she looked beautiful with her hair pulled back into a small bun. Martin wore a white shirt with no tie and crisply ironed chinos.

I love traditional rituals. It doesn't matter which religion, what gets me is the realization that these same procedures have been carried on for thousands of years; as I watch, I get a vision of peoples in earlier centuries doing exactly what is being done here, and I get a sense of continuity that I find both thrilling and comforting. Esther put a towel over her head and said a blessing over the candles. Martin said a prayer as he cut the freshly baked challah and handed a piece to each of us. Then he poured the wine into silver cups, said a prayer, and we all chimed in with the "amen" and drank.

The Jewish sabbath begins Friday night, which goes right along with the TGIF sense of relief that the workweek is over and let the good times begin. It's a festive occasion, and the three of us talked and laughed nonstop. I liked them, and their relationship was nice to be with: hers was total devotion and adoration, and his was a teasing fondness which she obviously enjoyed. By the time dinner and coffee were over, and I had helped Esther clear the table and put things away, it was ten-thirty and bedtime for all of us.

"What time is the trip to the Horta Museum tomorrow, Martin?" Esther asked. "Martin takes a group of handicapped children on outings every Saturday," she said proudly.

"Don't worry, darling," he answered. "You can sleep late—we're not going until two."

It wasn't too late to call England—there's an hour time difference, and besides, Murder Room Report Centres do not keep nine-to-five hours. He was there, as I thought he would be.

"Ah, the literateuse. Do I owe the pleasure of this call to friendship or curiosity?"

"Both, Superintendent. How are you and what did the autopsy and forensics find should about cover it."

He laughed, and I got the feeling he was sitting back in his chair for the first time that day. "I'm as well as I can be on a total of six hours sleep in two days. As Max said, the autopsy showed that she was garroted—and I don't mean strangled. This had the earmarks of a professional."

"How could you deduce that?" I asked.

"In most cases of strangulation, the murderer uses more force than is necessary and you find deep bruises and contusions. Our chummy here knew exactly how much strength kills, so there wasn't much damage to the internal and external structures of the neck. Very calculating and skillful. And the weapon looks like it was a piece of rope— probably with knobs at either end to help tighten it."

The garrote—an old Spanish message of execution.

"The other signs of a professional," he went on, "were that the only fingerprints we found in the house were yours on the outside doorknob and the downstairs phone. The place was wiped clean. Signs of a cunning, careful, and very cool bastard."

"No evidence of drugs in the body?" I asked.

"Drugs. What makes you ask that? Was she a user?" he asked quickly.

"Not that I ever heard. I was just curious."

"She had sexual relations a short time before her death, and she had ingested a full breakfast an hour or two earlier."

"Don't tell me—ham and eggs," I said.

"Right. We found the remnants of the ham roast in the garbage. So lover boy was probably there. The neighbors all reported seeing Islamic-looking men around often. The bus driver from High Wycombe says he frequently brings such men to the village who get off at the victim's corner. But no one remembers seeing any other men."

"It could be a man who has reason to be very discreet about their meetings. Remember she never let Anwar meet him," I said. "Either a man who's married, or someone who is a known local figure." I paused. "I assume you've checked on Hugh Eddington's whereabouts during the critical hours."

"No need to teach your grandmother to suck eggs, Ms. Rhodes," he said dryly. "Mr. Eddington has yet to offer any convincing explanation of his movements. He seems to think that being an executive and possibly next head of SATCOM LTD. exempts him from the need to provide us with an accounting of his time. And while we're talking about validating whereabouts, the postmistress remembers you well. Which is too bad. You make such a perfect perpetrator. A stranger who comes to the village claiming to have an appointment with the victim, who plies the postmistress with questions about the victim, displaying an inordinate interest in her. And then, lo and behold, she discovers the body. It's a perfect case, and if Max's autopsy hadn't definitely established time of death when you could not possibly have been there—I could pack up and go home tomorrow."

"I apologize for not being the murderer, and for keeping you away from home. Your wife must have a rough time of it with you away so much."

"She did, which is why I'm no longer her husband. I've been replaced by a nice, predictable stockbroker who never misses dinner, birthdays, and anniversaries."

"Has anyone ever done a study on the rate of divorce among detectives as compared to other professions?" I asked.

"I'd guess we would top the charts. It's inevitable," he said. "The job requires the kind of commitment that necessarily puts a wife and family in second place. Not many women can handle that."

"Doctors' wives do."

"Yes, but they have such lovely compensations.

Doctors' wives have social status and security. Being a cop's wife carries no cachet and no money. It's a great deal easier to handle the fact that your husband puts his career ahead of you when you drive a Jaguar and live in Surrey."

"Maybe you've been looking for a wife in the wrong places, Caleb. A woman with a career to which she's equally dedicated wouldn't be resentful. In fact, she'd be understanding and maybe even relieved not having to feel guilty about her own commitment."

I could hear the smile in his voice. "Do writers become committed to their careers?"

"Sometimes." This writer's role is getting to be trouble. I might have to play it straight with Caleb. But not yet. If the various branches of the British police force were loath to share information with each other, what chance did an unofficial American have? Thinking of me as a writer, he could indulge me without feeling threatened or compromised. It's only in books that the police appreciate the help of amateurs. Can you just imagine the Chief Commander of the London Police getting on national television to announce the apprehension of the latest Jack the Ripper and attributing it all to the smiling amateur sleuth standing next to him?

I thought it a good time to change the subject. "Did you get anything more from Anwar?"

"No, but he may prove helpful later in identifying the lover. Even though he never saw him, there may be something about him that Anwar can recognize. By the way, I never did hear how you made mugs of us by finding the boy while my men

combed the village, High Wycombe, and the bus
and railroad stations."

"The police follow protocol in a search," I said.
"I followed instinct. It seemed to me that a teenager
from the Middle East who has been dropped down
into a small English village would be too scared
and inexperienced to take off for the big unknown
city. My guess was that he had probably found a
secret hiding place for himself—and those old
buildings were rife with secret caches. I knew he
worked in the Church Loft, so I just walked around
it until I spotted a break in the roofline and knew
there had to be an access door somewhere."

"Ms. Rhodes, have you ever thought of going
into crime-solving as a profession?"

Boy, is he going to feel like a jerk when he finds
out what I do for a living. But I have an idea how
to cushion the blow when I ultimately tell him. We
chatted a bit more and ended the conversation with
my assurance that I'll see him at the coroner's inquest, which he expected would take place the following week.

XIII

I WAS AWAKENED the next morning by Esther knocking at my door. She looked pale and ill.

"What's the matter?" I asked in alarm.

"I have one of my PMS migraines," she said, speaking with great difficulty. "Do you think you could go along with Martin to help him with his outing? I usually go, but today"—she put her hand up to her head in pain—"I just cannot."

Martin and I met the children at a school for the handicapped in Uccle. Their name for him was "Monsieur Le Rouge" because of his red hair and beard, and they obviously adored him. We got them on the trolley that took us to the Rue Américaine, where the famous Victor Horta had lived in a simple town house which he transformed into a stunning tribute to his unique artistry. We helped the children move around the many levels of the marvelous house that is filled with curved arches, stained glass, and burnished woods. Not only did Horta do the architectural design for the house, but all the furniture as well. Everywhere you look are intricate decorative designs and carvings—on walls, doors, and furniture. Unlike many architects who tend to compromise design for comfort, Horta included many details that contribute to easier living. The children got a special kick out of finding a small sink hidden behind a hinged panel in the master bedroom. They were quiet and respectful as Martin explained how Victor Horta founded the Art Nouveau movement at the beginning of the century, and their faces filled with pride when he pointed out that Horta's architectural and design genius had given Brussels the international fame it deserved.

As we stood in the magnificent dining room, I saw two dark Arabic-looking men ascending the staircase and I stiffened. Then I looked at the children milling around me and thought, Relax. Who would try any mayhem in front of all these witnesses?

I noticed them following us as we got on the trolley for the return trip and my self-reassurance crumbled. Actually, I don't believe witnesses constitute a deterrent to criminal activity. As I remember, it took them hours to get the blood off the wall at Umberto's Clamhouse when Joey Gallo was splattered in front of a roomful of diners.

I took a seat along the side so that no one could sit behind me. I may have seen too many Clint Eastwood movies, but I could just see the bus driver, at the end of his route, coming over to wake that last sleeping passenger only to notice a large knife projecting from her back. The two men took seats opposite me. The hell with this cat-and-mouse stuff. I smiled at them, leaned over, and asked, "Didn't we run into each other while having Egg McMuffins last Ramadan?" They stared at me in shock—I don't know if it was because I had insulted them by suggesting that they'd committed the horrible sin of eating pig meat, during the Moslem holiday of fasting, yet—or because I confronted them unexpectedly. Of course, maybe they were just innocent tourists who didn't understand English and figured I was the kind of weird wacko their travel agents had warned them about. Or perhaps they were some of the thousands of illegal aliens who have flooded Brussels, and I could have yelled, "Immigration!" and gotten the same effect. Whatever, it worked. They hurried off the trolley at the next stop.

I didn't mention the episode to Albert that evening when we met for dinner at the Confessional on the Chausée Waterloo. It's not a monastery, it's a restaurant that has become one of my favorites in the area because they make a great waterzooi, which is that creamy chicken stew that is one of the tastier Belgian national dishes. We ate in the garden in the back—it was a lovely evening, and after consuming a bottle of Veuve Cliquot champagne, we were feeling dreamy and mellow.

The waiter brought our dessert of Poire Helene. I'm not big on pears, but I'll eat anything slathered with that marvelous Belgian chocolate. I was slowly licking the spoon, with the half-closed-eyes look of enjoyment I get whenever I savor chocolate. I was too rapt to notice the effect my display of sensual pleasure was having on my dinner partner until he nearly leaped across the table to kiss me, chocolate mouth and all.

"Emma, I adore you. Will you marry me?"

I had never seen it coming. I was so stunned that I actually stopped eating my Poire Helene. However, it didn't take me too long to collect myself to deal with the situation. It's one I have run into with sufficient frequency to have evolved a whole patter and behavior pattern. I don't want to be married. I don't want to share my life with anyone, nor do I want to share anyone else's life. I don't want to have to answer to anyone or have to alter my activities in order to please, or at worst, not irritate any man. I have been told that when you're in love, you feel you want to spend the rest of your life with this person. Well, I've been in love many times—but I never saw it as a forever thing. It was great, thrilling, romantic, even ecstatic—and then it ended. I understand from married friends, who may have been stretching the truth as do many people who want to convince themselves of the rightfulness of their position by pulling you into it, that this euphoria changes into something sweet and solid and grows into a wonderful, comforting bond. From my experience, it merely ends and all I'm left with is a nice feeling of friendship, if it ended well, and disgust if it didn't.

However, I'm only thirty-five, so I'm not ruling out the possibility that I will someday meet a man with whom I develop the kind of warm, wonderful, and everlasting feeling they talk about. However, dealing with the here and now—Albert isn't the one.

So I gave him my "I care about you but" Spiel

Number One. This is when I don't want the relationship to end. If the man isn't important to me, I just call the whole thing off, that's Spiel Number Two. Both routines are handled with delicacy and sensitivity that conforms with the Emma Rhodes' Code of Morality, which is: Never consciously hurt another human being. I'm sure that I may have hurt some people in my life, but it was never done intentionally.

I told Albert that I had feelings for him, that I loved being with him, but marriage between us would never work. It was fairly simple because in Albert's case the logistics alone would make marriage impossible. He had to live all year in Brussels, and I am constitutionally unable to stay in one place 365 days a year. Besides, how could I maintain my profession in Brussels alone?

"But you wouldn't have to work if we married, Emma," he said earnestly. "You know I have enough wealth for you to stay home."

"And do what?" I asked. "You don't need the money, Albert, and yet you work. Why?"

He looked at me with astonishment. "But a man must have a meaning to his life, he must be active and a contributing member of society. A man is defined by what he does."

Ye gods, the man is living in the nineteenth century. But I am not about to give him a lesson in understanding the current woman. I find that efforts to alter a person's point of view are futile and only result in an erosion of the friendship. And I don't want to end ours. I find Albert charming, entertaining, intelligent, attractive, and highly satisfactory in bed. In other words, he meets all my

needs of the moment—and let tomorrow take care
of itself. We ended the discussion with my not clos-
ing the door to his proposal, but saying that the
time is just not propitious for such a decision. Then
we went home—to his home.

XIV

SUNDAY IS NOT always a day of rest for a policeman, so Albert went off to work next morning, and I wandered around his apartment. It's in the chic area called the Sablon in downtown Brussels that consists of Le Petit Sablon on one side of Rue de la Régence and Le Grand Sablon on the other. It's the preferred address for the well-heeled arty crowd, wealthy people who prefer to be associated with creativity rather than the conventional social big-bucks-charity scene. They're the kind who spend millions on SoHo lofts in New York City, flats or houses in Chelsea in London or the Left Bank in Paris. The Sablon has beautiful ancient buildings that have been gutted and exquisitely modernized inside. Albert occupied a two-floor duplex apartment in one of those buildings, which I later learned he owned. It was expensively furnished in what I call Modern Macho, which means he turned the task over to a male decorator who lived out his fantasies at Albert's expense. The place abounded in purely functional chrome, steel, and leather, and there wasn't a comfortable chair in the house. There was no place to sit back and read a book, no comfy spot for a short snooze. The only inviting-looking seating lured you into sinking a foot down into a pile of soft leather contoured to be totally unacceptable to the human body and from which it took you ten minutes to extricate yourself. The bedroom featured a raised platform which elevated the bed to monarchial status. The only part of the place I liked was that which could not be touched by the decorator—the art. Albert had a marvelous collection of paintings, original lithographs, and sculpture. Matisse, Rouault, and Sam Francis glowed from his walls. Louise Nevelson, Rodin, and Giacometti were represented on pedestals and tables throughout the apartment. Even though he was a policeman, or maybe that's why, he had an elaborate alarm security system guarding the premises.

I made myself a cup of coffee in his state-of-the-art espresso machine and then went back to my hideout home-away-from-home.

I greeted Esther, who was doing her weekly laundry, and then went to my room just in time to get a phone call from England.

"Good morning, Caleb Franklin here."

"And a good morning to you, Caleb Franklin there."

"I rang to tell you the coroner's inquest will be Tuesday at 1400."

"Where?"

"At the Town Hall in West Wycombe."

"I'll be there." I hesitated a second. "Don't go

away, Caleb. I'd like to ask you something."

I could hear him smile over the phone. "I'm not going anywhere. What is it you want to know? I'll be happy to satisfy your curiosity, as long as it doesn't require my giving away classified state secrets."

"Caleb, I know this question may sound slightly off-the-wall, but I'd appreciate if you would just humor me. What were the companies whose executives had been kidnapped and the dates of their kidnappings?"

He read off the names and dates—and I checked them against the list of phone numbers (all of which I'd already called, of course) and dates on the card in Silvia's safe. They were the same.

"When this Naji contacted the families of the men kidnapped, was it a woman or a man who called?"

"A man."

Silvia had a partner. Was he the one who had killed her? And if he was, why didn't he take the money from the safe before he left? Could it be that she never gave him the combination? That would mean he trusted her but she didn't trust him. Or perhaps the murderer was her lover but not her partner and he knew nothing of the contents of the safe.

"Were the kidnappings similar in any way?"

"In most respects, yes. All of them were executives whose companies do business with Iran. They were known to make frequent trips there."

"The timing—how do you think the kidnappers knew when they were coming and where they'd be?"

"The knowledge could have come from either end. Anyone dealing with these men here in England would be privy to their travel arrangements and equally so in Iran."

"But what's in it for the kidnappers? Since The Naji retrieves them without ransoms being paid, he's the only one who makes out."

"We have thought of that," Caleb said dryly.

"Then you must suspect that these episodes have been setups by The Naji to collect the bonus, and that the kidnappings are bogus."

"But they are real. We questioned the victims and each tells the story of being taken at gunpoint by men who blindfolded them and kept them in a hot, damp room. They were threatened with execution if the ransoms were not paid; they were shackled and generally mistreated and frightened."

"Thanks for the information, Caleb. All I can say at this time is this knowledge may help me to help you solve the cases."

"Another of your Jane Marple insights that will make me the hero of Scotland Yard and the Foreign Office?" he asked.

"Too late for that, you already are."

I hung up and tried to put some of the pieces together. My deal with Felippa was that I would have her husband back safely within two weeks— that's fourteen days. Four days have gone by and I'm nowhere. And just to make things more complicated, a murder and a bunch of kidnappings have been tossed into the mix.

Time to call Abba.

"What's up, *Chamoodie* my love, any more attempts on your life lately?"

"Why ask me?" I asked. "You probably know more about me than my best-friend-in-blood Gracie knew when I was ten years old . . . and we told each other everything. I wanted to talk to you about what I think is some kind of conspiracy involving a mastermind and an Islamic group."

I could hear his ears prick up over the phone.

"The Partisans of God you mean?"

"Yes. I think they're being manipulated into committing all sorts of crimes for a Professor Moriarty who goes under the name of Naji and has his own dangerous agenda."

I told him about the kidnappings and the evidence of complicity in Silvia's safe. As I saw it, the kidnappings had to be orchestrated by someone who had contacts in the higher echelons of the British business world and was able to keep tabs on the comings and goings of top executives. All the men were doing business with Iran, and our mastermind knew just when and where they were arriving.

Abba snorted. "That's easy. You call for an appointment and the big shot's secretary says, 'No, Mr. So-and-so will be in Iran then, but he'll be back Tuesday.' How many good hotels do you think there are in Teheran? You think it's like New York City? You make a few calls, that's all."

"Then all Naji has to do is alert his terrorist groupies and they do their stuff. They send their ransom letter . . ."

". . . which he writes, since those Partisan cocksuckers are probably illiterate."

"He contacts the executive's company calling himself Naji, the savior, and offers to get their man

back as a humanitarian gesture except that he'll
need 200,000 pounds just to cover expenses. They
jump at the bargain—it's only ten percent of what
the kidnappers are asking, and the figure seems
reasonable, they're businessmen and they understand the need for bribery expenses in Middle East
negotiations."

Even if a company deep down doesn't feel their
man is worth two million, they have to be concerned about image. After all, it might hurt company sales and depress their stock if the public
learned they were allowing their executives to be
popped just because they're loath to part with a
couple of measly millions. So Naji becomes known
as Public Savior Number One, the Lone Ranger,
and Batman all rolled up into one romantic figure
when he's really an evil bastard.

"The beauty part of his scheme," said Abba, "is
that he's probably paying those Partisan *putzim
bubkes*."

"You're right. They don't know how much he
collects; all they know is they have to snatch a man,
hold him and scare him for a few days, then Naji
comes and picks him up and they get a fistful of
cash to buy arms for their cause."

"What a scam. Nobody even gets killed."

I reminded him of the two men whose murder
drove Felippa's husband into hiding. And then Silvia.

"He must have a golden tongue, or whatever, to
have convinced a woman like that to be part of his
plot," said Abba.

"She may not have known everything about him,
or chosen not to," I said. "People in love frequently

develop a convenient deadening of all brain functions other than sexual."

"Maybe she stopped thinking with her gonads and that's why he killed her. Something had to make him freak out—you don't eliminate a valuable partner without a damned good reason."

"I'm going to get this guy, Abba," I said firmly. "He's personally killed three people, destroyed the life of Bernardo and his family, and Lord knows how many other lives with drugs."

"Don't get too altruistic, sweetie—you'll lose your edge."

"Don't worry, Abba. I have 608,000 incentives to keep me at it. This may not sound like much compared to Naji's take, but it pays the rents."

"That's my girl. Righting wrongs is a wonderful thing, but I've seen guys get hooked on it, and they either end up dead or living out their lives in hand-me-down suits."

XV

MONDAY MORNING WAS one of those perfect cloudless blue sky days when the air is so clean and clear that you forget man invented the gasoline engine and expect to see only horse-drawn wagons in the street. Before I get carried away romanticizing the "good old days," I must remember that trying to keep your skirts clear of horse droppings when crossing the street and spending hours of rump-bumping wagon travel to go ten miles couldn't have been any picnic.

I decided to take a walk. Notice I didn't say I wanted to *walk*—that's fitness stuff where you're so busy swinging your arms and taking your pulse that you never get to notice let alone enjoy the scenery. I wanted to *take* a walk—that's strictly pleasure.

I came back thirty minutes later, walked in the door, and was suddenly set upon by a bushy 250-pound apparition who clutched me to his hairy chest.

"*Bubele*—you're still as gorgeous as ever."

"Abba!" I said joyfully after disentangling myself. "What are you doing here?"

He looked at me sadly. "You're not happy to see me?"

"Are you kidding? I'm ecstatic."

"You see?" he said, smiling broadly as he turned to the man who had come up behind him. "I told you she adores me. Emma, baby, meet Asher Cohen, one of my colleagues."

A red-haired, red-bearded giant clasped my hand. "I've heard a good deal about you, Emma." He had a firm handshake, freckles, and the greenest eyes I had ever seen.

"Come on into the living room," said Abba, leading us into the large light room that took up the entire length of the house. I noticed he went over to a far corner where three chairs had obviously been set up. He took the one facing the door, Asher took the one facing the window, and I sat in the middle.

I looked at Abba fondly. The thin black hair on his head was compensated for by the bushy mustache and beard that covered the entire lower half of his face. He had a broad turned-up nose, a great smile, and dark brown eyes that always seemed to be shooting sparks; everything about him exuded energy and enthusiasm. In all the years I have known him, I have seen him furious, loving, sad, and happy; the only way I have never seen him is apathetic.

"Where's Esther?" I asked.

"Oh, she had some errands to do. She'll be back later."

I saw we were operating on the need-to-know basis. Obviously Esther was not in the loop.

"Enough of the small talk," Abba said after settling his girth comfortably. "Asher is our Iran specialist. He knows your Partisan *shmuckim*. Tell her."

"They've never been a real group, you know. They've always been just a raggle-taggle bunch of layabouts and hotheads who like to make trouble because they have nothing else to do to fill their days and establish their manhood."

"You mean they're not really dangerous?" I asked.

"They're not connected with the Islamic Republic, which is one of the big sponsors of terrorism. And up to now, they had no real organization. But from what Abba tells me, they now have a leader— and that could make them dangerous."

"Do you know Bernardo Sandoval?"

"The Spanish archaeologist? Yes, he's visited Israel many times. He's highly regarded by our people."

"You know he's in hiding because they think he's responsible for the Israeli killing of two of the members of the Partisans of God."

He nodded. "We heard they put out a contract on him, as your American Mafia call it."

"Then you probably also know that I'm trying to establish his lack of complicity in the killings, which means, as I told Abba—was it just a few days ago—that I must come up with the real killer."

"Correction, my love," said Abba. "It's different than it was a few days ago. Now *we* have to find the killer. Why do you suppose we made the trip here? I was dying to be with you, of course, *sharmuta*, my love, but the Israeli government doesn't subsidize the mating *meshugas* of its employees."

Asher leaned forward. "If they now have a leader, as you've learned, and he's helping them buy arms—we have to get involved."

Abba snorted. "Who do you think they'll use those arms against? The ayatollahs can't fill their bellies, so they fill their minds with hate. Hate for America, hate for Israel."

"From the brief outline I got from Abba, this new leader knows exactly how to use that hate. But he's using it for his own personal benefit. That makes it easier for us."

I must have looked puzzled. "It's the zealots who are truly dangerous and hard to stop," Asher explained. "Their fanaticism makes them almost inhuman; they fear nothing, not pain, not death. In fact, death is a privilege if it is for Islam. But people who are in it for the power and the money, they have the usual human weaknesses, which means they're vulnerable."

"So, my darling Emma, the guys in the white hats have arrived to help. How about telling Asher the whole story from the beginning."

So I did. I have said many times that I prefer to work alone. Abba is my exception. He is an invaluable resource with incomparable skills, experience, and knowledge that I am fortunate to have available. More than that, he is totally reliable, discreet, and incorruptible.

Asher listened intently and did not interrupt me once. He nodded when he heard familiar law enforcement names like Albert Heist and Caleb

Franklin. I omitted nothing; I covered personal relationships, but of course not intimate ones.

When I finished, Asher got up and walked
around.

"So, it could be Eddington, it could be Don Luis,
it could be Don Roderigo."

"Then you don't think that Silvia's murderer and
Naji are the same person?" I asked.

"Yes, I do. What makes you think I don't?"

"Wouldn't that eliminate Luis and Don Roderigo? She was murdered by her lover."

Asher looked mystified, and Abba let out a howl
of laughter.

"I don't believe it. The sophisticated, world-
traveled Emma Rhodes. What's the matter, you
never heard of incest? You find it inconceivable
that a brother would have sex with his sister or a
father with his daughter? I can't even ask what century you're living in because, if Greek tragedies
were accurate, family-fucking was stylish in B.C.
days."

My retort was going to be that if he had met the
cast of characters, he would see how impossible the
idea was. I know that seemingly straight and
proper people can indulge in some rather unconventional sexual practices. I learned that in Rye
High School when Tommy Dunn, Sybil Rice, and
Janet Alden got suspended after they turned in
their highly detailed "How I Spent My Summer"
essays to Mrs. Robbers, the English teacher, whose
sexual experience didn't run to a ménage à trois on
Bleeker Street.

"Trust my instincts on this one, Abba—incest
would be out of the question in this family." I

mused for a moment. "You know, it's possible that Silvia's lover had left before the murderer arrived."

Asher looked puzzled. "What do you mean?"

"Because the bed was still unmade, the police assumed she had just completed lovemaking when she sat down to do some postcoital coiffure arrangement at her dressing table, and that her lover came up behind her to do her in. Maybe she was a sloppy housekeeper; the sex might have been over hours before and she just hadn't bothered to strip the semen-stained sheets yet. Lover might have left at nine and the murderer might have arrived at ten."

They were intrigued with the new possibilities. "The lover might have also been her partner in the Naji scam, which would account for the fact that the ransoms were untouched in her safe," I continued. "Why take it if he left on lovey-dovey good terms?"

"Wait a minute," said Asher. "Maybe *she* was The Naji."

"Men from a macho culture would let a woman lead them?" said Abba. "I doubt it."

"Mrs. Bhutto, Indira Gandhi, Margaret Thatcher—and how about Golda Meir?" I asked.

"As a matter of fact," said Asher, "the Partisans have a number of women in their group. It's possible."

"If she was the leader and also The Naji, then our troubles are over," said Abba. "Ho-ho, the wicked witch is dead."

"But not mine," I said. "If Silvia was the leader, how will I be able to convince those Partisan yo-yos that she and not you Israelis offed their brethren after Bernardo's tip-off? They'll keep up their vendetta against him forever.''

"And just to throw another curveball into all this brilliant theorizing, what about that disk full of company names you found hidden in Silvia's computer that shows that Eddington is in this up to his ass?'' added Abba.

"I feel like that juror on the O. J. Simpson trial who quit because she said there were 'too many clues.' ''

Abba got up abruptly. "Children, I suggest we do what I always do when my brain gets stuck. Let's eat. I hear there are great restaurants in Brussels—and we're here on my Mossad expense account. So where to, Emma?''

I took them to George's Brasserie because the food is good and plentiful, both prerequisites for Abba. He appreciates fine fare, but only if there's a lot of it. I will never again take him to one of those haute cuisine, "white plate" establishments. I call them "white plate" because the food is usually artistically (a euphemism for sparsely) arranged in the center of the plate, surrounded by sprigs of julienned whatever; all you see is a lot of white plate and a little bit of food. The only time I took Abba to such a restaurant, he looked down at the dish placed before him, looked up at the waiter, and asked:

"What is all this shredded shit?''

The waiter kept his polite cool. "Those are julienned vegetables, sir.''

"If Mr. Julienne is in the kitchen,'' said Abba, "kindly ask him to come out here and show me exactly how I can get this stuff into my mouth. You can't spear the suckers with a fork, they're too tough and skinny, and you can't get 'em on a spoon because they're too long. If they're here strictly for decoration, take 'em back and bring me roses. At least those I can put in a vase and enjoy them.''

The waiter came back in minutes with a plate of assorted vegetables.

We started lunch with *crevettes grises* fritters, which are made from the delicious gray shrimps that abound in the North Sea. They had carbonnade, the hearty Belgian stew, with three steins of beer. I had a salad and a glass of white wine. I ended with coffee; they each took two selections from the dessert trolley.

Abba will never discuss business during a meal. Given the kind of talk such work engenders, I don't blame him if he wants to preserve his digestion. We spoke about everything; these were two highly intelligent men who could converse on any subject. We touched on sociology, anthropology, history, and of course, the favorite Israeli topic—politics.

When we returned to the house, they plopped down in the living room. I looked at them splayed out on couches in a postprandial stupor.

"Now I know why you Middle Easterners need two hours for lunch. One hour in the dining room and one hour in the recovery room. I'm going upstairs to powder my nose and check my messages."

I turned on my machine and there was Felippa.

"Emma, dear, I know we're not supposed to bother you, but something has come up and Tía and I would so much appreciate it if you could come to tea at four today for just a small chat."

I never give progress reports; I let my clients know that from the outset. Since I'm not paid by the day and indeed may not be paid at all, they have no hold on me and I have no responsibility to them. That's the way I like it. However, this was by way of being a royal command, so I would have to make an exception. I phoned and told her that I'd be there. There was a "just calling to say hello" message from Albert that didn't require an immediate callback. I returned downstairs.

"So what time are you going to have tea with the queen?" asked Abba.

"You nosy bastard! You listened to my messages? That's a violation of privacy."

Abba laughed. "No kidding. Listen, tootsie, in my business I listen in on phone calls, I open people's mail, I bug their houses, I even monitor their fucking. Checking out answering machines was part of my basic training. By the way, your Belgian detective sounds like he has the hots for you."

I laughed and sat down. "Abba, you're incorrigible."

"You hear that, Asher? I can't be corriged. O.K., Emma, you go off to your tea. I'm going to take a short nap and then we're flying back. We have enough to go on and things to do. I'll be in touch."

XVI

THE QUEEN, FELIPPA, and I sat in that same lovely sitting room in the palace sipping coffee. This time the queen didn't even ask my patisserie preference but merely prepared a waffle and chocolate plate for me. They were both very upset about Silvia's murder.

"She was always a rather difficult child," said Fabiola, "but very bright and with, I think, a good heart. This is a terrible ordeal for Isabella and Roderigo. My heart goes out to them."

"Thank goodness it happened in England. If it had happened here, it would have been all over the newspapers and given them even more pain," said Felippa.

"Who could have done such a terrible thing?" said the queen. "Some lunatic, I assume."

"You read about such things," said Felippa, "about burglars breaking in and killing innocent people, but somehow you don't expect this to happen to someone you know."

Obviously they don't know the real story which meant either Isabella and Roderigo don't know or don't want anyone else to know, which is foolish because ultimately everything will come out. Murder cannot be kept private. After the coroner's inquest tomorrow, the sordid details of her death and the prurient circumstances will surely catch the attention of some opportunistic journalist, and the fact that the victim was a member of the aristocracy and a relative, no matter how distant, of a queen, is bound to get headlines that will top the tabloids at supermarkets everywhere. And then how would Fabiola and Felippa handle the fact that Silvia was in some way connected to the gang that was persecuting Bernardo? It's a mess and not one I care to step into.

The door at the far end of the room opened, and a liveried footman came in and announced to the queen, "Madame, Inspector Heist wishes to speak to you."

Albert—what is he doing here?

He walked in and bowed slightly to the queen, and nodded to Felippa and me.

"To what do I owe the pleasure of your visit, Inspector?" the queen said smilingly.

"I just wanted you to know, ma'am, that we are changing the times of the guard detail we have for Dona Felippa and Juan. I have made all the arrangements."

"I am sure that will be fine, Inspector. But you didn't have to come all the way here to tell me that yourself." She looked at him looking at me and her eyes twinkled. "But I do appreciate your concern. Thank you."

After he left, they both turned to look at me with that cat-who-ate-the-cream smile.

"I think the inspector did not really come to see me," said the queen.

"He's a lovely man, Emma," said Felippa.

"And from an excellent family, Emma," added the queen. "You mustn't wait too long for marriage, Emma—especially when you wish to have children." Her eyes clouded. The fact that she and Baudouin could not have children had been a great source of unhappiness to them. "He would make a fine husband, I think."

I can't believe it. It's enough that I got this kind of nagging from my aunts and married cousins, now a queen is telling me I'm not getting any younger and I should be gathering husbands while I may. I'll never understand what satisfaction people get from pairing people. Seems to me the risk isn't worth the effort, because if the marriage ends up in the dumper you end up losing two friends.

"Felippa, what was it that you wanted to talk to me about?" I asked.

Felippa drew a letter out of her pocket and handed it to me. "It's from Bernardo. He says he is all right."

I held the letter in my hand and looked at her. "If he's all right, how come you look so troubled?"

"He says he's fine, but I am not to try to find him or have anything to do with the Partisans. He is worried for me and Juanito."

I didn't bother to read the letter. "First place, I don't have to try and find him, I already know where he is."

Felippa and the queen gasped.

"Secondly, you are not involving yourself with the Partisans—I am—not only to save Bernardo's life but mine as well."

They both looked stunned. "What do you mean?" the queen asked. I told them about the threat that now hung over my life and the attempts that had already been made. They were aghast.

"*Madre mía*," said the queen. "Your life is in danger because you saved Juanito! How terrible that you are being punished for doing a kind thing."

Felippa reacted more like I did—she was furious. "Why those . . . those . . ." She would've loved to have said sons of bitches or worse but was restrained by the presence of her aunt.

"Emma, go to it. Men are always so protective of women, they treat us as though we are made of porcelain and have no minds at all. Do what you have to do, you have my support."

"And my blessing," said the queen.

As I was leaving, I asked, "By the way, may I see the envelope? I want to see who the letter was mailed to and what was the postmark."

Felippa shook her head. "The envelope will tell you little. It was not mailed—Luis found it in his diplomatic pouch this morning. There is no postmark or address."

XVII

TUESDAY—THE DAY of the inquest and Day Six for me. I rarely notice the passage of time when I'm working on a case because I'm too busy digging out facts, then analyzing and resolving the situations to bother to observe the clock or the calendar. I find people pretty simple to read and motivations fairly predictable and almost always I wrap the whole thing up long before two weeks. But this case has become so convoluted with unexpected elements that it has developed into a delicious challenge. As you can probably tell, I'm having a ball, which gives me twinges of guilt since one isn't supposed to derive pleasure from the misfortunes of others. However, I tell myself that I'm not responsible for Silvia's death, or Bernardo's and Felippa's suffering. And while we're on painful truths and brutal introspection, I admit to having become wired by the same factor that must hook all those marginally existing private eyes—danger! I'm stunned myself—me, Emma Rhodes, who has always regarded white-water rafters as crazy geeks, mountain climbers as slightly demented, and people who get a charge out of putting themselves in life-risking situations as mindless idiots who deserve the rough waters and avalanches that wipe them out. But I must admit that my two deadly encounters and the threat of more have turned me on. And the pressure of having to perform and resolve the case within the next eight days has become exhilarating. Which only goes to show that you may think you have a real fix on who you are now—but to quote Yogi Berra, "It ain't over till it's over."

The place was packed. The inquest was held in a large room furnished in Early Institutional with rows of green folding chairs and a table in front for the coroner, who had a small head, a large mustache, and heavy horn-rimmed glasses.

It looked like the whole town had turned out. This was big doings in West Wycombe; they probably hadn't had a murder since the eighteenth century. Since the victim wasn't one of them, they didn't have to be somber and sympathetic with grieving relatives, thus the inquest was even easier to enjoy. The postmistress waved to me, and I wondered who was handling stamp sales. Inspector Thornley, Detective Sergeant Parnell, and Dr. Ogilvy were in the front row along with Caleb and Sergeant Jarvis. I got a big smile from Anwar, who was in a rear row.

A murmur ran through the room as Luis arrived together with Miss Ballard and Hugh Eddington. He saw me and they all came over and sat next to me.

"I'm glad your parents didn't come," I said to him.

"They wanted to, but I told them they had nothing to contribute and it would be too painful for them."

The proceedings were routine. Inspector Thornley told his story and Dr. Ogilvy gave his medical report. There was a collective gasp in the room when he used the word "garroted." Caleb was treated very respectfully when he added his findings. Another murmur went through the crowd when my name was called, and as I walked up, I noted the postmistress making points among her fellow villagers by proudly being able to identify this mystery woman.

I wore my black Donna Karan power suit and a white silk blouse. I had spent a few minutes inspecting my wardrobe that morning to make my selection. Miss Manners offers no guidelines as to proper garb for inquests, so I was on my own. I figured you can't go wrong with basic black. I recounted the details of finding the body, to which the coroner listened carefully as he kept rubbing his mustache, as though it was fairly new and the novelty had not yet worn off. (Just a small note to impress you with my constant powers of deduction.) No questions were asked of me so I left the stand and sat down.

The verdict was "death by persons unknown."

As people were filing out, I felt a hand on my arm. It was Hugh Eddington.

"Miss Rhodes. Would you like to have lunch with me?"

I looked at him in surprise. I had sort of figured

I would grab a bite with Caleb and pick his brains
a bit. But having lunch with this smarmy oppor-
tunist and finding out what makes him tick suddenly seemed more intriguing.

"I'd love to," I said with a smile. "Let me just
say my hellos and good-byes and I'll meet you outside."

Caleb's eyebrows went up when I told him with
whom I'll be lunching. "Just as well," he said. "I'll
be eating at my desk today. And maybe you can
find out more about the elusive Mr. Eddington
than we have. He claims to have been home ill all
morning of the critical day—no witnesses, of
course. Says he wasn't sick enough to call a doctor,
and since he lives in a fashionable area where people specialize in minding their own business, he
can't offer collaborative testimony from the usual
nosy neighbors who gladden the heart and make
life easier for us cops. He phoned in ill, but that
proves nothing."

"I'll see what I can find out." He started to leave.
"Hold it a minute," I said. "I meant to ask—what
about the decorators who were in and out of Silvia's place? That Mr. Desmond who left his card."

He smiled broadly and pointed to a short, very
fat man with a wispy white mustache and watery
blue eyes who was just lumbering past us.

"Mr. Desmond?" I asked. He nodded.

I shrugged and left.

I've always found that a man's car defines his
self-image. Hugh had an Aston-Martin, the car
James Bond drives. It figures. We drove to a smart
little bistro in High Wycombe where everyone
seemed to know him. The proprietor fussed over

us and the waitress came right over with a smile—
and it was "Hello, Mr. Eddington!" all over the
place. He reveled in the attention. There are people
to whom this recognition is so important that they
rarely dine where they're not known. Since all it
takes to win this solicitous behavior is a frequent
currency-packed handshake with the maître d' and
lavish tips all around, I could never understand the
pleasure. But then I'm not burdened with the insecurity that requires that kind of sanctimonious
stroking.

When someone has the obvious need to be a
cognoscente, I always ask him to order for me. It
feeds his sad little ego, and I like to make people
happy as long as it doesn't cost me anything. Did
I ever press the right button! Hugh positively
beamed and assumed the responsibility of making
the dining decisions as though he was planning the
Battle of Waterloo. He conferred with the proprietor about what was the freshest fare of the day,
how many hours ago the fish was caught and how.
I must say I had a hard time keeping a straight face
when he asked the maîtred' whether the fish was
caught by line or net. I figure by the time they
slather all that sauce over it, who will be able to
tell if someone knocked the poor fish over the head
or shot it? I sat back and watched the conference;
it was obviously something both of them enjoyed
immensely, and who was I to scoff at another's
pleasure choices? I saw him glancing at me reprov-
ingly as I stuffed myself with bread and butter. I
knew I shouldn't be doing anything to diminish
my appetite and thus my full potential enjoyment
of the food, but I was starved. However, I re-

deemed myself by refusing a cocktail, which of course dulls the taste buds, and opted for an aperitif, which supposedly sharpens them.

When the ordering ritual was completed, he turned his full charm on me. He was good-looking, if you like the type, which I don't. Tall and pencil-thin (I prefer a little more meat on my men), he conveyed the effect of a man who took excessive care of his appearance. Another sign of insecurity, thank you, Dr. Freud. He had blue eyes that seemed to move constantly, as though never certain that his current situation couldn't be improved. His carefully razor-cut, blow-dried hair had touches of premature gray at the temples. His tan suit was pure Saville Row; he looked to be in his early forties. Women could find him attractive. The question is—did Silvia?

"I know you don't like me," he said.

I'll say this for him—he didn't wait for any protestations, which is just as well since he wouldn't have gotten them.

"Perhaps I come on strong because I care too much."

I waited. For what and for whom?

"If you knew something about me, perhaps you would understand why my career is so important to me."

It's not Silvia, it's the promotion. He obviously thinks I have some influence that will affect his taking over her place. O.K., let's see the performance he puts on to convince me that he's the man for the job. There would be no point in my telling him that my opinion in the matter would mean squat to Luis and his father since their business is not my bailiwick. But hey, a man must do what he must do, and I'm up for a show anytime.

He spoke slowly, in his well-modulated public school diction voice.

"I grew up in Wolverhampton in the Midlands. It took me years to get rid of the accent and learn to speak as though I attended Eton. We were very poor, and I vowed that I would never end up like my father."

Ye gods, this type of self-humbling admission from a man like Eddington must mean he's looking for some big-time favor. What on earth does he think I can do for him that is worth these soul-baring revelations?

His parents owned a small grocery shop and the family, consisting of him and his older sister, lived above the store. He hated his father whom he felt was exploiting and victimizing his mother, whom he adored. Since her husband was shiftless and ir-responsible, she was forced into the backbreaking twenty-four-hour-a-day job of running both the business and the home.

"When I was fourteen, I came home from school one day and found my mum lying unconscious in the store. As usual, our dad was at the pub, so I ran to the neighbors, who called the ambulance. She'd had a stroke, she couldn't talk or move, the doctors didn't know when or if she would ever re-cover, so she was moved to a National Health home where she stayed for four years. I would go every day after school and sit by her bed to tell her everything that was happening in my life; I just knew she could hear me. I worked hard in school because she had always told me that education was the only way to escape from poverty and get ahead in this world. When I was eighteen, I bicycled to the hospital as fast as I could to tell her that I was to be graduated first in my class. I knew she'd be proud of me. When I arrived, they told me she had died that morning."

He stopped for a minute to recover himself. I felt my eyes tear. If this guy was acting, he outclassed Olivier.

"I never went back home."

He got a job that earned him enough money to go to the United States and apply to M.I.T., where he was accepted as a scholarship student. "I wanted to go into computers because I knew that's where the future moneymaking was. I didn't have the style or connections that would get me ahead in the business world in England; I needed to do something where one is valued by skill and ability only."

"Did you ever see your father again?" I asked.

"No," he said stonily. "I hated him—he killed my mother."

"And your sister—what of her?"

He smiled. "Oh, yes, we're in close touch. She's a wonderful woman. She lives in Portugal. She turned her house into a home for abandoned children. In poor countries like that, people who can't afford to feed their children often just drop them off anywhere. Can you imagine that? She takes them all in and cares for them."

A change came over his face as he talked about his sister. Love and pride drove away the pinched unpleasant look of venality. Maybe there's hope for him yet.

"Where in Portugal does she live?" I asked.

"In a little town you probably never heard of in the Algarve. Silves."

Actually, I knew it quite well since it's a short drive from my house in Vila do Mar. I also know that the sad tradition of the poor abandoning their children is a carryover from the oppressive days under the dictator Salazar when extreme poverty was rampant. Yet the Portuguese government makes adoption by foreigners almost impossible since they see it as a blow to national pride to have their children removed from Portuguese soil. It's the same stiff-necked stupidity being displayed today by Russian politicians and other governments who care more for their own national images than for the welfare of infants who are being denied the right to be brought up in loving homes rather than grim institutions.

"Does the state support her operation?" I asked.

"Very little. I finance her," he said simply.

I began to feel I'd misjudged the man. It wouldn't be the first time I had made the wrong conclusion from a first impression. Of course, it could also be that he was the no-goodnik I thought but just had some good qualities. I understand that Hitler was wonderful to his mother. And Attila was a loving daddy.

He went on to recount that after graduating summa cum laude from M.I.T., he worked in California for a number of years until he became a leading figure in Silicon Valley and internationally known in the computer industry.

"I wanted to come back to England—but I wanted them to come to me—and they did. SAT-

COM LTD. was—and is—the leader in software in the UK. They offered me a vice presidency and here I am. I always intended to be the chairman one day; I still do."

"But when Don Roderigo bought the firm, didn't you think you might have to change your plans? Especially after he put Silvia at the helm?"

He smiled. "Not change, merely readjust. I knew that in time my importance to the company would have to be considered and eventually I would reach my goal."

"Of course Silvia's death will accelerate your timetable," I said.

"Not if I'm held guilty of the crime."

Aha. Now I know why I'm here. Not just for my influence over Luis and Don Roderigo, but because he believes I have the ear of the great Detective Chief Superintendent Franklin. He wants me to be his double-duty do-gooder. Fat chance, sonny boy.

"Where were you the morning she was murdered?" I asked. If he wants me to put in a good word for him, he'd better get me clear on the facts. Now I have every right to interrogate him.

But unfortunately the fish arrived at that moment and we had to devote ourselves to the deboning process because of course it was cooked with the bone in. True gourmets say pfah! to fillets because their purist palates dictate that bones give the fish its full flavor. Which means unless the waiter debones it for you, you must do the job yourself. It's really not difficult once you get the hang of lifting up the center bone. Never mind that it puts a real crimp in your table conversation because you must be ever vigilant for those little side bones that can require the Heimlich maneuver. We labored in silence until the job was done.

"I was home ill," he said as soon as he could speak.

"With what?" I asked.

"I'm afraid I overindulged the evening before at dinner with a customer."

"You mean you had a hangover?"

He looked a bit sheepish. "I'm not used to drinking hard liquor. My drink is wine, but the customer was a double malt drinker, and I had to go along with him. I barely managed to get home that night and couldn't move in the morning. I phoned the office, told them I would be in later, and just popped off to sleep. I woke at noon, had some coffee, and went to the office."

"That sounds reasonable to me, but unfortunately there's only your word. The police like substantiation. You realize you had an excellent motive."

He threw up his hands in seeming despair. "What can I do to prove I was at home? I made no phone calls, I received no phone calls—I was asleep. Does it help to tell you that I cannot kill anything—that any insects I find in my house I carry outside?"

"All that means is you'd make a lousy entomologist."

"I respected her ability, and there was room for both of us in the company. Why would I kill Silvia?"

"Maybe it had something to do with the project you two were working on together, you know, the stuff you were looking for in her computer."

Bull's-eye. He turned the bright red that troubles all fair people who try to hide their emotions.

"That had nothing to do with anything." He stumbled a bit. "That's just some hush-hush idea we had for a new product."

Right. If it was bona fide company business, why did you look and act so guilty then and now?

Suddenly his face took on a crafty look. "But I hear Silvia was killed by her lover."

I don't know how he had heard that, but news seems to have a life of its own in villages. One of the police force might have mentioned it to his wife, in strict confidence of course, and she got it out on the drums the moment he was out of the house. Actually, all she'd have to do is mention this juicy tidbit to our good lady postmistress and it would be all over town within an hour. After all, her job is to handle village communication, isn't it?

"Why would the fact that she was allegedly killed by her lover preclude you as a suspect?"

He looked astonished. "Surely you jest," he said. "Look at me—do you think someone like me would ever take someone like Silvia to bed? Why, the woman was a pig!"

Whatever happened to *"de mortuis nil nisi bonum"* and whatever happened to Mr. Nice Guy? As to whether I think he would make love to Silvia . . . I think he'd sodomize King Kong if it would help his career.

"Look, Hugh, I'd like to help you, but how can I? The police weigh the facts—that's all they have to go on. When it comes to motive, you're way up there. When it comes to alibi, you're way down there. All you can do is wait and hope they find the guilty party soon. My telling Superintendent Franklin that you're a self-made man who is good to his sister might make him think kindly of you, but it would have no effect on his classifying you as a possible suspect."

He looked crestfallen. "But doesn't character count for anything in his considerations?"

It sure does, Buster, which is why your name heads the list. I marveled at the man's blinding self-involvement. How delusionary could a person be? This totally amoral bastard sees himself as an upright sterling individual. Next he'll be telling me that he sang in his church choir. He's the kind of person who has no compunction about committing the most corrupt deeds and dishonest transactions and passing it off as "but that's business."

I thanked him for lunch and asked him to drop me off at the railroad station. Then he surprised me again.

"Would you like to meet my sister? She's visiting me at the moment. I know she'd enjoy meeting you and I think," he said with a note of pride, "that you would like her."

Why not? She sounds like a neat lady, and besides, I'd like to get a peek at Hugh's flat. A man's home may be his castle, but it's also a barometer of his character as well as income.

It wasn't a flat—it was a house, a small jewel of a villa surrounded by the archetypal English garden that owes its glorious colorful perfection to loving care and the ideal rain-plus-sun British climate. I liked Elizabeth Eddington on sight; you couldn't help it. She was a slight, birdlike woman with bright brown eyes and hair worn in a careless bun kept somewhat in place by bobby pins. A black shawl similar to the ones worn by Portuguese fado singers was draped over her shoulders. Her face projected caring, warmth, and unqualified acceptance of all human beings. You were instantly comfortable with Elizabeth because you knew you were not being judged and she was prepared to like you. I felt I had known her all my life. When I told her I have a house in Vila do Mar, she was delighted and we lapsed into Portuguese until Hugh pleaded with us to revert to English.

The love and respect they had for each other was lovely to see.

"I don't know what we would do without Hugh," she said, looking at him proudly. "His money keeps us going, but I worry that he deprives himself."

Not to worry, Elizabeth, this lad will always take good care of his needs. I'll bet his idea of deprivation is to be forced to eat a piece of unripe Brie.

"He hasn't bought a new piece of furniture for this place since he moved in," she said earnestly. I looked at the seventeenth-century French desk that stood in the entry hall, which I recognized from the Sotheby's sale two years ago when my offer for 100,000 pounds was passed over, and looked at Hugh who gave me one of those little what-can-I-say shrugs. The house was furnished with exquisite pieces and displayed its owner's fine taste and full pockets. Obviously Elizabeth was far removed from the scene of worldly goods; her concerns were only in the areas of worldly good.

She told me that she was in England on a fund-raising mission and was planning to go to Brussels in a few weeks. "I'll be staying at Hugh's flat."

"Oh? Hugh, I didn't know you kept a flat in Brussels."

"Yes," he said. "SATCOM has constant dealings with the EC and I'm there so often, I find I need it."

I told Elizabeth to call upon Diane Reed, my hostess in Brussels, who is a wonderful, compassionate woman and might be able to help set Elizabeth in the right fund-raising directions. I gave her the phone number and address within full hearing of her brother. If Hugh was involved with the Partisans of God, by now this information would be nothing new to him or them.

When Hugh drove me to the train for my trip back to London, I told him how much I liked and admired his sister. His face was suffused with pleasure.

"Elizabeth is a saint," he said with deep emotion. "I would do anything for her."

That's what I am afraid of.

XVIII

~❦~

I SPOKE TO Peter Drury and made the calls to set up my appointments for my trek to visit two of the companies whose executives had been kidnapped and returned.

Peter and I were what was known as an item five years ago, but it sort of petered out (pun intended; it was the expression used by all his former lovers.) His full name was Lord Peter Drury, Duke of Warrington, with a lot of letters after it. As the first son, he inherited the title and a vast estate in northern England ten years ago. Like many of the big landholdings that had been in families for hundreds of years, everything was crumbling around their inept titled heads. But fortunately for the Drury family, Peter also inherited the shrewd brains of his maternal grandfather, who had made a fortune in supermarkets. Within a few years, the young lord managed to bring the estate around into a highly profitable position without having to turn it into a tacky circus like Woburn Abbey. Once that was accomplished, Peter became restless and looked for other uses for his keen financial brain. He bought a small magazine called *Financial Forecast* that was big on theories but very short on readers and profits, and built it into the most highly respected publication in the UK. When I wanted to meet with the CEOs of major companies on such short notice, I knew the only way of getting appointments would be calls from on high—and Peter was about as high as you could get in this area.

We have remained very good friends, as I do with most of my former lovers. With one or two unnotable exceptions, one in which I had to threaten the guy with a court order to keep him away, and one in which the man actually dumped me (it took me three months to get over that indignity), all my relationships end with warm but no longer hot feelings for each other. My reasons are simple: I don't like unpleasantness or hurt feelings, and you never know when an ex-lover can come in handy.

Peter knew what I did, of course. As a matter of fact, he had referred a few cases to me when some of his titled friends needed very discreet resolutions to some highly embarrassing and sometimes dangerous situations.

When I gave him the names of the corporations I needed to see, he merely phoned the CEOs and told them I was a journalist to whom he had assigned the writing of a story on corporate security required when sending executives to do business in Middle East countries. There's no company head in the country who would not take a call from Lord Peter, and who would not be highly flattered to be the object of interest by Peter Drury, publisher of *Financial Forecast*.

At six a.m. Wednesday morning I was on the M40 on my way to Chipping Camden in my rented Rover.

I usually try to avoid the motorways, but this time speed and not pleasure was the purpose. I have two hair-raising handicaps to overcome when I drive in England: the first is adapting to driving on the left side of the road, which usually results in my mounting a few sidewalks in town and wobbling over center lines on the highway. The second is entering those ghastly British inventions called "roundabouts," to which my reaction is to sit paralyzed until I work up the nerve to swing into the dizzying swirl of traffic coming at me from all directions while trying to ignore the honking of horns behind me.

I moved on to the A40 past Oxford and into one of my favorite areas in Britain, the Cotswolds, with all those lovely "on" towns like Stow-on-the-Wold, Shipston-on-Stour, Bourton-on-the-Water, and of course Stratford-upon-Avon. I had not been a devotee of Shakespeare, because he was imposed upon me in high school by an inept and inarticulate English teacher, until I saw John Wood in a modern-dress *Julius Caesar* in Stratford and found myself standing and applauding wildly when the curtain went down. I love staying at the Lygon Arms in the nearby little village of Broadway, but only out of season because it has become the favorite of American travel agents who recommend it to clients who are "doing the Shakespeare country." There are four-feet-thick walls, a four-poster bed with the year 1620 carved into it, floors that aren't quite even, and a hidden stairway.

I arrived in Chipping Camden and followed the given directions to Cellubell Ltd., which is the largest manufacturer of cellular phones in the UK. It was located on the main roadway slightly out of the town. I found a spot marked VISITORS that was right next to the slot marked JOHN CRICHTON that was occupied by a gray Bentley in the totally full parking lot. When I got off the elevator on the third floor, I realized why the place was in such an out-of-the-way location: to keep away stockholders who might rightfully become incensed at seeing the lush extravagance of the executive offices. The two-inch-thick carpeting and obviously hand-blocked wallpapers prepared me for John Crichton, founder and CEO of Cellubell. Experience has taught me that self-made men like to surround themselves with blatant testimonials to their successes, like ballroom-sized private offices fitted with executive W.C.'s equipped with Jacuzzis and gold fixtures. Crichton's office was a classic case in point. He greeted me warmly and led me across a deeply carpeted expanse to the informal grouping seating area furnished with silk-upholstered wing chairs and an authentic Chippendale coffee table. This positioning augured well: I was in the VIP area. The usual setup in these offices that must make a statement is a three-part division of space: the Desk for his important decision-making work, the Conference Table for presiding over subordinates, and the Informal Area for meetings with those evaluated as his peers. After he made sure I was comfortable and had a place to set up my tape recorder and notepad, he smiled and said, "Well. Sir Peter said you were very able, but he forgot to mention that you were also very beautiful."

I was wearing my purple Louis Feraud suit, which is one of my male G.C. outfits—that stands for "gender correct." Men and women may be equal, but they have different tastes. Take food, for instance—even with today's nutrition-aware eating consciousness, men will grumble if served salad as the main course at business luncheons, while women usually prefer it. And clothes—women will admire another woman's outfit if it's smart, but men only notice if it's flattering. When I'm working, I factor in appearance as an important element in my performance. If I'm dealing with an older man, I know they enjoy seeing a pretty woman, so I dress in feminine, softly colored clothing. Younger men see me in more hip outfits. And women get the smartly coordinated and stylish parts of my wardrobe. It sounds calculating, and it is. Why not? If you plan your pitch before going out to make a sale, shouldn't you also do everything possible to insure favorable reception of that presentation? If a certain type of appearance eases your way and helps insure the success of your campaign, why the hell not do it? Actually, I detest shopping for clothes, but since I consider them part of basic artillery for my campaigns, I'm forced to hit the stores periodically. Unfortunately, the IRS doesn't agree with me and won't allow me to deduct clothes from my income tax. I don't know why: I bet they permit Diana Ross to deduct hers. About every six months, when I get a twenty-thousand-dollar fee I go to my hometown in Rye and blow the whole bundle in Reitmann's, a store that has designer clothes at discount prices. It sounds ridiculous with all the money I make that I should be looking for discounts, but chauffeured limos drop off customers at Reitmann's daily, and if these obviously loaded women can go looking for bargains, why not me? Besides, I like to spend money but I don't like to waste it. If I can get thousand-dollar suits and eight-hundred-dollar dresses for half price, it makes my day. I divide my search into smart suits for women clients, flattering dresses for men clients, and sporty casual shirts, skirts, and pants for me.

John Crichton was obviously an unenlightened male chauvinist, but I was not here to alter his philosophy, only to get information. We chatted about the tremendous success of his company, and I delighted him by mentioning all the cellular phone users I encountered throughout London, without of course alluding to the irritating intrusive element they have introduced to city life. Then I got to the kidnapping, but not before I had turned down two offers of tea. It's a lovely English ritual, but it's time-consuming, and time is what I don't have today.

"Our people have all been trained by an industrial security expert I hired just to prevent such kidnappings," he said. "We do business all over the world, and we've had some unpleasant experiences in South America, but never before in Iran. So perhaps Tom wasn't as alert as he might have been. But the way it happened, I don't know if anyone or anything could have prevented it."

"What were the circumstances?" I asked.

He got slightly uncomfortable. "Well, you see, he has this male problem. You know, prostate. So he goes to the men's room fairly often." He was a bluff man in his early sixties, of an age that found it embarrassing to discuss personal physical details with a woman. "He was eating in one of the good restaurants in Teheran. All he remembers is walking into the bathroom. Apparently someone was waiting for him, knocked him unconscious, and got him out someway without being seen."

"The ransom note asked for two million pounds?"

"Right. We would have paid it, of course. Tom Preston is our vice president in charge of marketing and very valuable to this company."

Not to mention to his wife and family. The statement had a hollow ring because in reality this man didn't believe anyone other than he was worth tuppence to his company. Self-made men tend to discount the importance of subordinates and feel that everyone is dispensable except them. However, he's too shrewd not to realize the unfavorable PR that would result if he left an employee to molder and probably eventually be murdered because he was loath to part with an amount that would be paltry to his company.

"But then I got this call from that chap who calls himself 'The Naji'."

"What did he say?"

"Claimed to be an antiterrorist. Said he had lived in Iran for many years and knew his way around. Said he detested what these savages were trying to do to British business, he knew ways to rescue our man, and all he wanted was ten percent of the ransom, not for himself but to pay off certain people there."

"And you believed him?"

"Well, he sounded like a gentleman—spoke the right way, if you get what I mean."

Of course, public school upper-class diction would have a strong impact on the self-made John Crichton.

"But don't get me wrong, Miss Rhodes. I didn't get where I did believing every bugger who can dial a phone. He said he believed in fighting injustice and it was an Englishman's duty to help his fellow countryman if he can. Well, I'm as patriotic as the next man, but those days of putting your life on the line for God and Empire are dead as yesterday's tea bags. So I figure the man's got his own angle and 200,000 pounds isn't tin and maybe it doesn't all go for expenses. If there's a chance of getting Tom home, and saving 1,800,000 pounds to boot, it's worth a shot. You can't build a business like this without taking some risks along the way. So I decided to take this Naji chap up on his offer." Then he assumed a cunning look. "But I set some of my own terms. Told him I'd be daft to pay him in full up front, what with him having no track record at all to prove he could pull off what he was promising. I offered to pay him half now and the balance on delivery."

"And he accepted your terms?"

"He'd be a dim lad if he didn't," he said indignantly. "It were a reasonable piece of business negotiation."

"How did you make the payment?" I asked.

"Oh, real hush-hush, cloak-and-dagger stuff." I

could see he really relished the whole adventure. "He told me to put the money into a Marks and Spencer bag and give it to a woman in a black dress who would be sitting in front of a certain locker at Victoria Station at ten o'clock the following morning. I did as I was told."

"What did she look like?"

He shook his head. "Hard to tell. She wore those flaming big sunglasses they wear these days and a big hat pulled down over her face. I dropped the bag in her lap and she didn't so much as look up, sat like a right statue, she did. I walked a few steps and turned to look back and she was already gone."

He smiled broadly. "And I was right, by God. We got Tom back all in one piece."

"How did he accomplish the rescue?" I asked.

"No point in your hearing it secondhand. Tom's right next door. I'll let him tell you."

He picked up the phone and called, and a few moments later, a tall, erect, gray-haired man in his fifties entered.

"Tom, this is Emma Rhodes. She's doing a story for Sir Peter Drury and wants to hear about your rescue."

We shook hands and he sat down in an adjacent chair.

"Well, there I was sitting on a stone floor, blindfolded, handcuffed, and shackled it seemed like for days. Suddenly, I heard the door open and figured it was one of the guards—there were three, I think. I heard someone whisper my name and tell me to be quiet, he was here to get me out. He had a funny accent, not like the others. He had gotten the key to my shackles somehow, and took them off quietly. He didn't remove the blindfold or handcuffs, and told me to be absolutely silent and get down on my hands and knees. I crawled as he guided me, and then we came to a wagon and he helped me in, then he pushed me down and we went on for what felt like two or three kilometers. Then he transferred me to a car and we drove for almost an hour. I heard sounds of people and music, and the car stopped. He took me out, stood me up, removed my handcuffs, and asked me for my word as a gentleman not to remove the blindfold for at least two minutes to give him time to leave. Said it would be deadly dangerous for me or anyone to see him. I did as told, and when I removed the blindfold, I was in front of my hotel."

"And here we have Tom with us right as rain, eh, Tom?" And he slapped him on the back. Tom smiled and went back to his office.

"Well, that's quite a story, Mr. Crichton. I congratulate you on your judgment," and I began packing up my equipment.

"And he's done it four more times, I hear. That Naji fella's got the kind of backbone and grit we don't see too much of these days."

You don't know the half of it. As I got up, I glanced at the computer on his desk and got a sudden hunch.

"You do business with SATCOM, don't you?"

"Aye. We use their systems throughout our company. Terrible what happened to Miss Lopez. She was a fine businesswoman, did a fair miracle in building up that place. But she was biting off more than she could chew, I thought, when she came asking for money for that fancy system product she wanted to develop."

I stopped. "She came to you for financing?"

"Yes. I didn't like to turn the little lady down, but I think she was way out of her league."

"Would you have thought so if she were a man?"

He was too secure to be even slightly bothered by the question. He laughed heartily. "Hell, no."

I have to admit, I liked the guy. I thanked him for his time and left.

I headed up past Coventry to pick up the M1 again that would take me to Sheffield and to one of the loveliest areas in England—Yorkshire. Fortunately, BIOBRIT LTD. was located just outside of the city so I did not have to fight my way through the tangled streets of that steel city.

David Chapman, head of BIOBRIT, was every inch the Harrow-Oxford man, as was quickly apparent by his regimental tie and the frequent allusions to his schooling that he managed to drag into the conversation. His biotech company had recently won approval for a handheld blood analyzer that had sent their stock soaring and had undoubtedly made Mr. Chapman an exceedingly wealthy man. His attitude about dealing with The Naji was very different from John Crichton's.

"If he hadn't phoned me, I would have found a way to reach him," he said emphatically. "The man is a marvel. I had no question that only he could save our man in Iran. Just look at what he's done. He manages to find where they're hiding and is clever enough to know just how to spirit the poor chap out of there."

"So when he asked for 200,000 pounds for his work, you didn't bat an eye."

"Not for a second."

"How was your man kidnapped?" I asked.

"John Branson is a jogger. They picked him up when he was making one of his morning runs."

"I'm surprised your security people didn't caution him against such solitary activities," I said.

"No need ever. John Branson is a black belt karate expert."

"Then how did they get him?"

"Chloroform. Two men."

The tale of escape was similar to Tom Preston's. As was David Chapman's opinion of SATCOM's services. I had decided to play my hunch again and asked him if they used SATCOM.

"Excellent organization. Their service and support for their systems is exemplary. We rarely lose a minute in downtime. Their consultant is here promptly whenever we need him. Shocking about Miss Lopez, fine woman."

I took another shot in the dark. "Yet you didn't want to get involved with financing her start-up project."

He shook his head. "My board would never have approved that kind of investment. I thought very highly of Miss Lopez—good family and all that—but her idea was just too blue-sky for us. We're a conservative company and we prefer dealing only in areas we know."

My next stop, which would be my final one for the day—I'd already crossed half of England—was Harrogate. I raced there as fast as possible to be sure I would still be able to make it in time for a Cream Tea at Betty's.

Betty's is a tearoom restaurant on the corner facing the park in the center of Harrogate. It's a large, many-windowed establishment where people wait patiently on line for the chance to enjoy the most delectable Cream Tea served anywhere in England. In case you're not familiar with this English specialty, Betty's version consists of two freshly baked scones, a small pot of strawberry jam which you spread on the scone and top it with a dollop of clotted cream which is in the second little pot on your plate, plus a pot of tea, of course.

After I had my tea, I phoned Alicia Bickley. My usual stay-over spot when I'm in Yorkshire is right outside of Ripon at the estate of my friends Alicia and Tom Bickley. It's a lovely place with rolling lawns, and sheep and cows grazing right outside the dining room. Tom inherited the home from his family, but the whopping yearly tax bill forces them to take in guests, a not uncommon predicament today among the owners of England's stately homes. I always find it amusing to see Alicia, who is a marquis's daughter and grew up not knowing a rolling pin from a bowling pin, now cooking marvelous meals and baking delectable pastries for the stream of strangers who pay her for her labors. When I phoned to say I would be coming, Alicia wailed that there was not a room available since they were expecting a six-couple invasion of Americans from Chagrin Falls, Ohio.

"You mean I packed my flannel nightie and woolies for nothing?" I exclaimed.

"Oh, Emma, Tom swears we'll get central heat-ing with the next bit of guest money. But by the time he pays the rates, and feed for the cows and sheep, we're stone broke again."

As long as I remember, Tom has been avowing a longing to dump the estate and settle into a nice warm centrally heated flat. But he is too deeply rooted in the place, and Alicia does enjoy receiving all the engraved invitations that are forever lined up on the fireplace mantle attesting to the Bickleys' popularity and social standing in the town where they are regarded as the landed gentry.

I checked in for the night at Caesars Hotel, which is a small place next to the lovely Valley Gardens. My trek also included companies listed on Silvia's mysterious disk and the first one was in Harrogate. In the morning it was pouring with rain, as is usual in Yorkshire, and I drove to the outskirts to find the first address. I passed the Conference and Exhibition Centre, which has contributed to the tax base and traffic of Harrogate, a mixed blessing. The address was Springfield Court, which was puzzling since this was obviously not a commercial area but was filled with Victorian houses of the forbidding stolid design that makes them look like clerical manses, built in the days when Harrogate was a popular spa. I was looking for Fairfield Ltd., 157 Springfield Court. When I came to the very end of Springfield, I saw what looked like a large garage that stood by itself. A handwritten sign bearing the number 157 was affixed to the front door. I parked in front, walked up, and knocked. There was no answer and no windows to peer into, so I walked up the steep front steps of the adjacent house and rang the bell. After a few minutes, the door was opened by an old woman with bright yellow hair, red lipstick, wearing a pink woolen jumper that looked about two sizes too small, and a cigarette dangling from her lip.

"Yes, dearie?" she asked.

It took me a few seconds to adjust to her hairstyle, which was cornrows with gray roots.

"I'm looking for Fairfield Ltd. and I was given the address of 157 Springfield Court."

"Well, dearie, you found it. That's it next door in our old garage."

"No one seems to be there," I said.

"Happens Mr. Thurston isn't about now."

"Who's Mr. Thurston?"

"Happens he's the gentleman we leased it to, let's see, been 'bout last June, I reckon."

"Who's that, Livvy?" I heard a loud voice call from the back of the house.

She turned and shouted, "It be a lady looking for Mr. Thurston."

"Well, tell 'er he ain't here. And where's me tea?"

"Does he come here often?" I asked.

"Who?" she asked.

I knew I'd better push this interrogation along because she was already suffering from braindrain.

"Mr. Thurston. Your tenant."

"Right on the dot, first of the month, he comes to pay his rent and pick up the packages."

"Who delivers the packages?" I asked.

"Why, postman, of course. I sign for 'em, locks 'em in the garage, and bob's your uncle, Mr. Thurston is here that very day. Knows exactly when they're coming, he does," she marveled. "Never use that old garage . . . no car since Alf smashed up the Austin comin' home from the Saracen's Head in the snowstorm of January '89, or maybe 'twas '88. I told him, didn't I, to walk, but he'd have none of it." She gave a cackle. "But now he has to walk everywhere, don't he? So there was the old garage, standin' there doing naught. So when this gent rings the bell one day and says he fancies it for his business, well, I'm over the moon." Suddenly she stiffened and eyed me suspiciously. "You not be from Inland Revenue or such?" she asked.

I assured her that I was not from any official organization.

I heard the shout for "Where's me tea?" again and she started to close the door. "Sorry, dearie, got to give old dad his tea." And she shut the door.

I drove to Nottingham where the next company on the diskette list was located and found the same setup—a blind. The next one was Northampton—the same.

All the names on Silvia's disk were for companies that were nonexistent. They were nothing but drops. But for what?

XIX

BACK IN MY "safe house" in Brussels, I suddenly became fed up with this fugitive existence. True, it hasn't hampered my activity too much, but I don't like the enforced vigilance I have been forced to develop. And I feel guilty that my so-called freedom is causing a strain on Abba's resources. I was about to phone him and tell him, to hell with all this Salman Rushdie stuff, I'm going to take my chances out there, when I heard a knock on the door. It was Esther.

"I heard you come in, Emma. Martin just came home and we thought you might like to join us for a late dinner."

Perfect timing—it allowed me to follow my life rule of never making any major moves while in the heat of passion or anger. I accepted with alacrity. As we came down the stairs, Martin was standing at the foot holding out two glasses of chilled white wine.

"What a man," I said with a smile as I took one. "Just what I needed."

He and I sat at the kitchen table sipping wine and munching on crackers and some sort of delicious eggplant spread while Esther busied herself with pots and pans. Martin smiled as he watched me load cracker after cracker.

"I think I detect an imminent request for a recipe, honey," he said to Esther.

"Oh, yes, please," I said. The stuff was delicious. "Is it complicated? You know, I never use any recipe that involves more than one half inch of ingredients and one quarter inch of directions."

"Not to worry, Emma. This meets your prerequisites," said Esther. "The ingredients are one eggplant, one large green pepper, and two medium onions. You just roast the eggplant until the skin bursts and the insides are mushy. Meantime you sauté the green pepper and onions. Then you put the eggplant mush plus the green pepper and onions in a food processor, add salt, pepper, and about two tablespoons of vinegar, and that's it."

"You either call it Bubby's Eggplant Schmear or Eggplant Caviar, depending upon to whom you're serving it," said Martin as he refilled my glass.

He looked tired, and I commented that he must've had a busy day and I hoped it was a successful one.

"Actually, yes, it was. I finally convinced a customer who I had been working on for months to go along with our thinking for his company."

"Martin can be very persuasive," Esther said proudly as she stirred a pot.

He walked over and put his arm around her. "I must be," he said. "I persuaded the boss's beautiful daughter to marry me, didn't I?"

She looked up at him and tweaked his red beard.

"That was hardly proof of your salesmanship, darling. You know I was always turned on by red-headed men."

What a cute couple, I thought. Suddenly I heard the phone ringing upstairs in my room.

"Damn it—I forgot to switch on my answering machine." I raced up the stairs in time to pick up the call.

"Emma, this is Elizabeth Eddington."

I heard the agitated tone in her voice. "What's the matter, Elizabeth?"

"I hate to bother you, but it's Hugh. I haven't heard from him and I'm worried. After you left this afternoon, he got a phone call and had to fly to Brussels immediately. He said it was urgent business and he would phone me when he arrived there. He should have arrived hours ago, and I'm afraid I'm a little frantic."

"Maybe he just got so caught up in the business meeting that he didn't get a chance to phone you," I said, trying to calm her.

"Oh, no, he would find a moment," she said emphatically. "He always has, it's a custom between us. You see, he knows I'm a terrible worrier."

"What would you like me to do, Elizabeth?"

"I hate to presume to ask you—but I remembered you were staying in Brussels, you gave me the number of your friend's flat, and I wondered if you couldn't just take a few minutes to run over to Hugh's place and see if he's all right."

"Sure. I'd be glad to. What's his address?"

She had the provincial person's concept of a large city. "Running over" to Hugh's apartment could take far more than a few minutes. Luckily, when she gave me the location, it turned out to be nearby in Uccle in a building near the Avenue Ha- moir. I went downstairs to tell Esther and Martin that I'd have to skip dinner. As soon as she heard why, Esther turned the flames off on all her pots and said, "Come on, let's go."

I protested. "Nonsense," she said. "It will take you a half hour to get a cab and you'd never find the place yourself if you took my car."

"You stay here, honey," said Martin. "I'll drive Emma there."

She looked at him and said firmly, "No."

He understood at once. I was her charge; this was her job.

It was a four-story building, and we had to ring for the concierge in order to get in. I pushed the "Eddington" bell a number of times and got no answer. We had obviously taken the concierge away from his favorite TV program and he was not in the best of humors, but I have never come across a concierge in the world who wasn't a grump. I told him the story and asked him to come up with us and let us into Hugh's flat. Of course, he balked. Two strange women walk in at night and ask to enter a tenant's flat—it was a battle. *"C'est urgent,"* I said. *"C'est possible que Monsieur Eddington est ma- lade, ou mort."* The *"mort"* stopped him for a mo- ment. But what finally got him was when I said that I would then have to call my friend Inspector Heist of the Judicial Police. I have learned that the only two things that get a concierge's attention are money and the word "police," and I didn't feel like blowing fifty francs on what I felt was probably a wild-goose chase. Reluctantly, he went back into his flat to fetch the keys and change his shoes. After all, one cannot engage in business wearing carpet slippers.

He knocked and rang the bell, and then opened the door. Esther and I followed him inside. Everything looked neat and tidy, and I called, "Hugh?" No answer, so I walked into the bedroom and saw a man asleep in the bed. I was just about to say, "Whoops! Sorry!" when I realized something about his position seemed odd. I stood there frozen for a second and felt a knot in my stomach. I moved closer to the bed. Esther was behind me when she heard my small cry. It was Hugh Eddington, but he wasn't sleeping. His face and neck were congested and were a dark red: there was a straight line bruise around his neck. I felt sick. I heard the *"Mon Dieu! Il est mort?"* of the concierge and a sharp exclamation from Esther that made me turn in time to see her turn pale and grasp the bed for support, and for her to see the tears in my eyes. Poor Hugh, poor Elizabeth.

An hour later Albert and I were sitting in the concierge's flat while the concierge's wife bustled about making coffee and sandwiches. It's not every day one has the chance to entertain a *Commissaire de la Police Judiciaire* and be involved in a murder, and she was reveling in the entire affair. Her husband was obviously depressed at the building management's certain accusations of his failure to maintain security, while she was delighting in visions of her certain social success as the insider who would be in demand at all teas, parties, and other local functions. Maybe she would even be in-

terviewed on TV, and wouldn't that twist the nose
of that stuck-up Madame Renaud who never let
you forget she once had her picture in the paper
when she won a cooking contest.

I had already performed the sad task of notifying
Elizabeth Eddington. She was flying over to identify the body, accompanied by Caleb Franklin,
whom I had phoned with the full approval of Albert. The similarities of Silvia's and Hugh's murders plus their business affiliation made a tie-in
between the two cases obvious. Although Belgian
jurisdiction prevailed since the crime occurred on
their soil, the cooperation that exists between fellow EC nations made an invitation to official British participation polite if not mandatory.

The door opened and one of Albert's men peered
in. "We're finished with everything, sir. The M.E.
wants to talk to you." A short, fussily dressed man
who reminded me of David Suchet's Hercule
Poirot came in clutching his black bag.

"Have a seat, Maurice," said Albert, "and tell us
all about it." He looked over at the concierge and
said with a winning smile, "M'sieur, could you and
Madame please step outside for a short while? I'm
devastated to have to ask you to leave your own
home, but as you can understand, this is official
business that must be discussed."

What a charmer. Most of the policemen I have
known would have just told the couple to bug off.
They bowed to him respectfully and left immediately.

"The time of death was probably between two
and three hours ago," announced the doctor.

"Rigor mortis hasn't even begun. And oh, yes, he's had recent sexual activity."

"She must be some hot number for him to have flown from London for the assignation," I said.

He eyed me coolly. "Why do you assume it was a she?"

This was a guy who got his kicks from shocking people, and from his smug smile, I gathered that the expression on my face thoroughly gratified his neurosis.

"There were semen deposits in the anus and on the penis. Your victim was homosexual, and if it weren't for the obvious professionalism of the garroting, I would have suggested death occurred as the unfortunate result of some aberrational sex."

I didn't bother to defuse the little man's bombshell effect by telling him that I am neither shocked nor bothered by anyone being homosexual. My feeling is that what people do in their bedrooms is strictly their business, and if I refrained from socializing with anyone who engaged in unconventional sexual practices I would have a very slim address book indeed. What shocked me was that, as a woman, I can usually sense a man's homosexuality and can tell if his disinterest in me is based on no chemistry between us or on the fact that he's just not sexually interested in any women. I didn't get those vibes from Hugh, which leads me to believe he was bisexual.

The little man arose and said, "Of course, I'll have more details after the autopsy."

After he left, Albert suggested we get to his office to meet Caleb and Elizabeth, who should be arriving soon.

When they walked in, Elizabeth came right over to hug me. We stood there wordless for a moment.

"Oh, Emma, I'm so sorry to have involved you in this terrible thing," she said.

She has lost her only brother, her whole world is crashing around her, and she's concerned about me. The woman is a saint.

"Who could have done this? Hugh was such a wonderful man, why would anybody want to kill him? What is this all about?"

It wasn't a rhetorical question—she really wanted to know. I didn't know what to tell her. She looked at me for a moment.

"Emma, you mustn't think because I've chosen a somewhat secluded life that I am naive and ignorant of the world. Hugh indulged himself in that misapprehension because it filled his need to be my protector, and I saw no reason to disabuse him of that notion if it pleased him. I want to know what was going on in Hugh's life that brought on this tragedy." She saw me hesitate. "Believe me, I am much stronger than you think. Please, tell me everything."

So I did. I could see that Albert and Caleb thought I was being a little too harsh and tried to soften some of the facts, but it was Elizabeth who stopped them. When I finished, she leaned over and kissed me.

"Thank you," she said simply. Then she turned to Albert. "When do you want me to identify the body?"

A policewoman suddenly appeared. "I'll take you, Miss Eddington."

Elizabeth looked at her and smiled. "That's Ms., please." And they left.

Caleb looked at me with a little smile. "So, Ms. Rhodes, for you another day, another body. We've established that you're not an innocent bystander and you're not a catalyst—what are you? You must admit it's a little strange that in less than two weeks you've managed to thwart one kidnapping and discover two murders. That's more mayhem than most people see in a lifetime, if ever."

"Maybe that's your answer, Detective Superintendent."

"What's that?"

"I'm just not 'most people.' "

"I think she has you there, Superintendent," said Albert, looking at me fondly.

Of course, Caleb caught the look immediately, and I noticed his sudden awareness of the existence of a relationship between Albert and me.

"There's no doubt of the connection between our two murders," said Caleb, now all business.

"Yes," said Albert, "but since one came about at the conclusion of a heterosexual episode and the other of a homosexual one, shouldn't we question the assumption of the lover being the murderer? Couldn't it be someone who knew them both well, disapproved of their immoral behavior, and entered the scene afterwards to punish them?"

"You mean like a sort of hand of God perpetrator?" Caleb said dubiously.

"Like Don Roderigo," I said.

"Don who?" asked Caleb.

"Silvia's father," said Albert. "I know him to be a very devout man and also very brave and physically powerful. He made quite a name for himself in the Spanish Civil War."

"On which side?" I asked quickly.

"Franco's, of course," said Albert.

"You're a romantic, Emma," said Caleb. "Did you think a member of the nobility would ever take the side of the Loyalists? *For Whom the Bell Tolls* was surely not for a Don Roderigo."

"If we're considering the family, Don Luis would be the natural suspect," said Albert. "*Cui bono*—who benefits."

"With both Silvia and Hugh dead, Don Roderigo would probably turn the running of the business over to Luis, or sell it outright, which would make both him and Luis very wealthy men," said Caleb. "I gather Don Luis is a bit of a playboy, which may mean the need for big money to maintain a profligate lifestyle."

"I don't know from where you gathered this information, Chief Superintendent, but it's inaccurate," I said. "First place, Luis is a working diplomat and a serious scholar. Secondly, I have never heard any rumor or seen any indication that he's short of cash."

"I think," said Albert, "that we must wait for the results of our forensics and postmortem before we conjecture any further."

"In the meantime," said Caleb, "it would be a good idea to check on the whereabouts of both father and son on the murder days."

I don't know about the father, I thought, but there's a bit of a shadow on the activities of the son on the morning of his sister's death.

XX

I WAS FAST asleep when the phone woke me, and for a moment I didn't know which home I was in, a difficulty encountered by those fortunate enough to be multi-home owners. Which is why, wherever I am, the phone must be next to my bed so that I don't run the risk of slamming into a lamp table near the window because that's where the phone is in New York. I have a friend whose husband woke up in the middle of the night in their London apartment after an evening of lavish booze consumption, turned left to where the bathroom was in their country home, and urinated against a French eighteenth-century armoire. The refinisher kept asking my friend, who refrained from answering for obvious reasons, what substance had stripped the furniture so drastically, thinking to learn of a new miracle chemical.

When I answered the phone, it was Albert. If it's Albert, this must be Belgium.

He was calling to tell me the results of the postmortem and forensics. I was astonished with the speed with which the work had been accomplished. Normally such reports don't come out for days or sometimes even weeks. When I mentioned my surprise, I could hear his hesitation.

"Aha, I detect the power of palace pressure," I said.

"Well, let's say the matter is of great concern to the family of our queen. Sometimes those considerations do cause us to accelerate procedures."

A model of diplomacy.

They found absolutely no fingerprints anywhere, not even Hugh's, which indicated a coolheaded pro who did a fastidious wipe-down of the premises. Just like Silvia's. The angle of the garroting showed the assassin stood above the victim. Since Hugh was six feet tall, he had to have been sitting or lying down when killed. There were no deep bruises, abrasions, or contusions on the neck usually caused by a murderer using more force than is necessary to kill the victim, which again indicated a professional assassin.

"Weren't there signs of a struggle?" I asked. "Hugh was very fit and would fight, I should think."

"There were no fractures of the hyoid bone or thyroid cartilage that occur in a struggle. But they did find a bruise on the back of the head that must have rendered him unconscious first."

I didn't like the guy, but I felt a flash of pity for him. As I said earlier, I am always pained by the sense of loss when a person is killed, and feel a deep anger directed against the individual who dared to think he or she had the right to end the life of any human being.

"Albert, I think you should make a comparison test between the semen match in Hugh and that found at Silvia's."

There was a second of silence. "What do you mean? You think the man who slept with Silvia was also Hugh's lover?"

"Albert, it may not be a fact that has played an important part in your life, but as a policeman I should think you'd have become aware that your male equipment is quite versatile. I think you ought to check with England to see if there's a match."

I could almost hear him blush over the phone.

"All right. I'll take care of it."

"Where's Elizabeth Eddington?" I asked.

"She wanted to stay in her brother's apartment, but of course we couldn't permit it. She's a brave lady."

"I think it's more a matter of economics rather than courage. She probably can't afford a hotel."

"That's all right. We put her up at the Hotel Archimede. The Judiciaire is paying because we require her presence for a few days."

We made a date for dinner, and then I phoned Elizabeth to meet for lunch.

I took her to a little bistro on the Avenue Winston Churchill that is a neighborhood rather than tourist restaurant so that we could have a quiet place to talk. We ordered quiche and salad and a demi carafe of the *vin de maison*.

"You know," she said as she sipped her wine, "I never resented Hugh for having left me with the

job of taking care of my father. He was devastated
by the illness and death of our mother, and I understood his need to escape. He had this driving
need to make good, as though to prove to Mum
that he could do her proud. And the moment he
could afford it, he began sending me money regularly."

"How long did you care for your father?"

"Twelve years. He died of liver cancer. By then,
I had lost the chance for marriage and babies. But
now I have dozens of children," she said with a
broad smile.

"What brought you to Portugal?"

"After our dad died, Hugh sent me money to
take a trip and I went to Portugal. I fell in love with
the Algarve, as everyone does, and decided I
wanted to spend the rest of my life there. I had
saved up a little money, so I rented a small house.
Then one day I came across a little girl tied to a
tree where her parents had abandoned her because
they couldn't afford to feed her. I took her home,
and that began my *Quinta do Meninos*—the House
of Children."

"Will you be able to maintain it now?"

She looked down at her glass sadly. "Oh, yes. I
spoke to Hugh's lawyer this morning, and he tells
me I am an heiress. My brother left a substantial
estate to me." She smiled ruefully. "A good part is
in a trust and that's my fault. Because Hugh
needed to feel he would protect me like he felt he
failed to do for our mother, I allowed him to believe that I was totally inept with money and he
handled all my finances. Actually, all the years I
took care of my father I ran the store and also had

an at-home accounting business for small stores in our area. I'm actually a whiz with figures. But there's plenty now for me and my children to be comfortable for the rest of our lives." Her eyes filled with tears. "The Lord moves in strange ways. Perhaps Hugh's death was meant to assure the future of the children."

Religion moves in wonderful ways. If it gave her comfort, how much better than being left with a sense of emptiness and total loss. Not for the first time, I rued my atheism and envied believers. Who knows? Perhaps someday I may change my views. I left her on Chausée Waterloo, where she wanted to shop for children's clothes, and we agreed to meet next month when I planned to be in my home in Vila do Mar.

I phoned Albert when I returned home.

"It's a match," he said. "The same person killed both Silvia and Hugh."

"No. The same person had sex with both of them—but that doesn't necessarily mean he killed them."

"You may be right, Emma, darling, but I'm afraid I don't have time to discuss the matter now. In fact, I'm afraid I must break our appointment tonight. Something very important has come up and I don't know when I'll be free."

Of course, nosy me, I had to know what was going on.

"A reliable source has informed us that a large drug shipment is coming into Brussels airport tomorrow night, the twenty-fifth, on the seven o'clock plane from Iran. We must be there, of course."

The twenty-fifth. Those phone calls to Silvia and
Luis.

At 6:50, I was standing behind a pillar where I
had a perfect view of Iran-arriving passengers. I
looked around and spotted Albert and his men,
who were scattered around trying to hide their
walkie-talkies and look natural. Suddenly my heart
sank. There was Luis. I wished this was a mystery
novel where it would turn out that the obvious suspect was not the culprit. But from what every cop
has told me, in real life the person who seems guilt-
iest is. I walked over to Albert.

"Emma! What on earth are you doing here?"

I started to tell him about Luis, but suddenly the
passengers began emerging from the gate. He held
up his hand to silence me as he turned to study the
procession. I watched the stream of people trudg-
ing out, some wearing that beatific "thank God I
survived" look and others the zonked mien one
gets after hours spent in an airless limbo. Most
were clutching some sort of luggage in sizes that
make you wonder if the airlines define "carry-on"
according to the strength of the passenger rather
than the size of the piece; a steamer trunk strapped
to the back would probably be acceptable. Some of
the passengers were obviously Iranians. A porter
pushing a woman in a wheelchair who was in a
full chador accidentally brushed up against a post
exposing her jeans and sneakers. Hmm, unusual
for a jeans-wearer to submit to the imposition of
this oppressive female garb. Especially when she's
out of range of the fanatic Iranian regime. The porter stopped to turn her over to a waiting friend

who started to wheel her away. It was a tall, chino-clad man with red hair and a red beard. I yelled to Albert and ran.

We all stood together in the office of the airline security department. Dr. Martin Hirshon was trying to explain that he was merely there to meet an old friend. The removed chador had revealed a dark intense young woman of about twenty, wearing a T-shirt that said HARD ROCK CAFE.

"Emma," he said in a friendly but puzzled voice, "what is all this fuss about? Mitra and I met years ago when I sold some equipment to her father's company. She's here to do some business with the EC."

"I thought dealings between Israel and Iran were prohibited," I said.

He smiled with that conspiratorial "we're all men of the world" look. "One can always get around such rules, if one knows where and how."

"Ma'am, may I ask why you are in a wheelchair?" I asked.

"She doesn't speak English," Martin said quickly.

"In what language do you and your old friend communicate, Martin?" I asked. "French? Flemish? Arabic? Farsi? Hebrew perhaps. No problem—we have all of these languages right here in this room."

"Well," he said in slight agitation. "She does have a little English."

"Good, shall I repeat my question?"

She looked at him and he nodded. "I had my leg blown off during the Iran-Iraq war by an American-made bomb," she said contemptuously.

Her English was only slightly accented.

I looked at her legs. "You have an excellent prosthesis," I said. But it looks a little large, I thought.

I turned to Albert. "Is there a policewoman here?"

"Yes, of course," he said. Then he took me aside. "Are you sure you know what you're doing?"

"I don't believe in coincidences. Tell the policewoman to look inside the artificial leg."

Martin lunged forward as if to protect her. "Why are you subjecting her to this indignity?"

I looked at him. "I left the note on the kitchen table telling Esther I was going to Bruges, Martin. Only she—and you—could have seen it. I left a note telling her when I was going to London. Only she—and you—could have seen it."

"What are you talking about, Emma?" he asked with a smile.

"Only you could have given my whereabouts to the Partisans of God."

I felt, rather than heard, a reaction from Mitra.

The tall blond policewoman standing by wheeled Mitra into another room.

"Dr. Hirshon, won't you sit down?" Albert said pleasantly. It was a bare room simply furnished with a wooden table in the middle surrounded by blue plastic chairs. He motioned for Martin to sit on one side while he took the head position and motioned for me to sit at his right. A uniformed policeman stood at each of two corners of the room.

"Would you like a cigarette, Dr. Hirshon?" asked Albert.

"No, thank you, Inspector. I have no bad habits."

"I think that remains to be seen, Doctor," Albert said with a slight smile.

"This is really quite an outrage, Inspector."

"That, too, remains to be seen, Doctor."

"I'm a respected businessman working with the EC. I have lived and worked here in Brussels for almost six years, and I think you will find not a blemish on my record."

I could see Albert getting a bit nervous. He was responding to my suspicions and was becoming concerned with their validity. I think he was beginning to worry that his hormones were affecting his judgment. The moments passed more slowly than usual until the door opened and the blond policewoman walked in and handed a note to Albert.

"The entire leg was lined with packets of cocaine, five kilos in all, street value of over three million Belgian francs," Albert said triumphantly.

Martin whistled. "Really? I had no idea."

"Didn't you really, Dr. Hirshon? You're just a kindly friend of the family who was here to help the young lady, is that right?"

"Absolutely."

"Martin," I said, "do you really think she'll keep her lips loyally sealed once she hears how much you've been taking out of this little operation compared to how much you've been giving them for the Cause?"

Obviously he did. The man truly believes he's irresistible. I motioned to Albert to step outside and I briefed him on the whole story—including The Naji and the fictitious customers on Silvia's disk.

"I think Martin is the head honcho of a drug operation throughout the EC," I said. "His business

takes him everywhere, so that it would be easy for
him to arrange contacts. Those bogus companies
are probably distribution centers; they were located
in the UK, Belgium, and France. It all fits—he built
up a cadre of blind mules to carry the drugs from
Iran to Belgium by fanning the fires of Islamic rebellion that's rampant in Iran. He speaks Arabic
and Farsi, too, so he had no trouble communicating
with the troops, telling them drug-running is an
easy way to raise money for arms. If Mitra is any
example, they're young, and one thing I'll say for
Martin Hirshon, he's smart and he's almost char-
ismatic."

"He's also ruthless," said Albert. "It will not be
easy to get any kind of confession from him."

"Why don't we start with the weaker link?" I
asked. "Mitra."

I asked for a more informal lounge setup rather
than the forbidding, austere rooms they have in air-
ports for official use, and we were given the use of
a small sitting room used by the chief of the airport
who was away at a conference. I could see that
under the attempt at brash bravado she displayed
was a very frightened young girl.

"Mitra," I said, "do you know the worth of the
cocaine you were carrying?"

She held her mouth tightly shut and did not answer.

"Dr. Hirshon will get over three million Belgian
francs for it."

Her eyes widened.

"How much of that is he sharing with you?"

Silence.

"It's you who's taking the risk, you know. You

were found with the drugs; Dr. Hirshon walks off a free man—there's no penalty for pushing the wheelchair of a smuggler carrying drugs. But you can end up with—Albert, how many years in prison can she get?"

"Anywhere from ten to fifty years."

A shiver ran through her. "The Belgian prison population has their own morality," said Albert. "Crimes are rated by them according to their own rules. They do not look kindly upon people who deal in drugs which may be sold to schoolchildren. It's difficult for prison officials to give any special protection to such prisoners. They quite often are murdered, and believe me, they do not have an easy death."

She was very frightened by now, but the loyalty of her fanaticism kept her quiet. I decided to try a more personal approach.

"Those two members of the Partisans of God who were murdered, you knew them?"

She finally spoke. "One was my brother, the other my cousin. The Israeli pigs will pay."

"But the Israelis did not kill them. Dr. Hirshon did."

Mitra gave a disdainful laugh. "You lie. Why would he do that?"

"Because your brother and cousin were smart enough to realize they were not getting their fair share of the drug money and that Dr. Hirshon was using the Partisans of God for his own profit, which has been exorbitant. You people are risking your lives with no other goal but to make him a millionaire."

She was beginning to waver. "Mitra, he is Israeli.

Didn't you ever wonder why he would help the
Islamic cause?''

"He despises the Israeli government," she said
with venom. "They make peace with Arafat and he
hates Arafat—as do we. We hate him because he
is a weak woman who is ready to lie down under
the heels of the Israelis because he is too old to
fight. And Martin hates him because he killed his
younger brother.''

I looked at her. "Martin never had a brother. He
is an only child.''

She looked at me contemptuously. "I do not believe you.''

Albert arose and motioned to me to follow him
out of the room. We walked out, leaving her in her
wheelchair under guard.

"I believe it's time to get back to work on Dr.
Hirshon. Let her sit for a while and worry and
wonder about what we told her.''

We went back to the room where Martin Hirshon
was sitting back in his chair. He looked totally calm
and self-assured. Albert looked at his watch and
turned to one of the uniformed policemen. "I think
Dr. Hirshon may be hungry, as am I. Why don't
you bring us, please, some sandwiches and coffee?''

He turned to me. "Just coffee for me, black,
please," I said.

"And you, Dr. Hirshon?''

Martin was obviously feeling very cocky. He was
able to read from our reaction that we were unable
to break Mitra and was starting to relax.

"I'd like a ham-and-cheese sandwich, please.''

I looked at him in surprise. "Ham! But you're kosher."

He smiled mischievously. "Only when Esther is around. Actually, ham is my favorite meat."

"Did you especially like the way Silvia cooked it for you?" I asked quietly.

I felt Albert stiffen beside me. Martin paled, then caught himself. "Who is Silvia? Is that a restaurant somewhere?"

"You were Silvia's lover, weren't you?"

"I don't know who you're talking about."

"Silvia Lopez, the head of SATCOM. There's no point in pretending you didn't know her, Martin. I think you did business with her company. It's easy to check."

His cool was slipping. "Well, yes, I did some consulting for them."

"Then you knew her," said Albert.

"Well, yes—but not in the biblical sense," he said with a grin.

"But that's exactly how you knew her, Martin," I said.

He snorted. "Ridiculous. I maybe ran into her once or twice in the office in High Wycombe."

"That may be true. But you also visited her in her home. You made love to her, and you killed her. Where did you learn to use the garrote, Martin? In the Mossad? Was that your weapon of choice when dealing with enemies?"

"Nonsense. You could never prove that. Are there witnesses who saw me there? Never. Besides, all that happened in England, this is Belgium."

"That's true. And this is Brussels, where you arranged to meet Hugh Eddington in his apartment, had sex with him, and killed him. The patterns are identical, the murder method the same."

"This is insane, first you accuse me of drug dealing, then murder, and now you accuse me of being gay. You know me, Emma—do I strike you as a homosexual?"

"No, Martin, you strike me as a man who would use any weapon he has to achieve his ends, if you'll pardon the choice of words. You needed Silvia, so you had an affair with her. Somehow you stopped needing her, so you killed her. You needed Hugh, so you had an affair with him. You stopped needing him, so you killed him."

He threw back his head and laughed. "Emma, you should be a mystery story writer. This whole thing sounds like something out of P. D. James. You're making wild allegations without a shred of evidence. I think I've had enough—and unless the Commissaire here has any other business, I'm going to leave." And he got up.

"Oh, but I do have a little more business, Dr. Hirshon. You see, we do have evidence that you were in both Dona Lopez's bedroom and Mr. Eddington's," Albert said calmly.

Martin sat down. He looked totally self-assured.

"You left your personal calling card in both places," Albert said. "Oh, you were scrupulously careful, I'll give you that. You came and went at times when no one was about. You wiped your fingerprints carefully off every surface. Except two. The bedsheets and the inner surfaces of the bodies of your victims. I believe a DNA test of the semen stains will show you were very much in Miss Lopez's and Mr. Eddington's beds, as well as bodies, just before they were murdered."

I was amazed to notice that Martin was comparatively unperturbed and quite self-contained. The man was being accused of three heinous crimes, his entire future and life were in jeopardy, and he acts like we're discussing what he ate for dinner last night. A famous criminal lawyer once told me he never liked to put a client on the stand because if he was innocent, he was so nervous that he came across as guilty, and if he was guilty, he couldn't hide it well enough. The only defendant who does well on the stand is a psychopath because his psychosis convinces him of his own innocence and makes him a master at conveying that to a jury.

"Martin," I said, "I like you. One can't help liking you. You're charming and you're very smart. You have everything going for you—a loving wife, a lovely home, a good business that will undoubtedly be yours someday. It's a life most young men only dream of. Whatever could drive you into this career of crime? The planning and methodology were brilliant. It seems to me that only someone with severe psychosis would risk tossing away this ideal existence to create such a network of intricate schemes of malfeasance."

I could see the wheels whirring in his head. He knew the DNA would be conclusively incriminating and more than likely we'd get a confession from Mitra. I had just offered him a defense that could save him, plus a heavy dose of admiration which he adores, and the irresistible opportunity to demonstrate his brilliance to the world. My years of experience in the care and feeding of male egos gave me the sense that this one would lap it up if it was laid on with a trowel.

"My dear Emma, risk-taking is the mark of the genius. Every high achiever in history has disregarded conventional wisdom and taken his own path. Salk wasn't afraid to work with live polio bacteria, Steve Jobs wasn't afraid to name a computer after a piece of fruit, Van Gogh wasn't afraid to paint according to his own vision. Well, I have my own vision, and like all geniuses, the means is merely servant to the goal."

I like the company he places himself in. Each of those men's achievements had a tremendous positive impact on the world, while our raving redhead's aim is solely to produce power and big bucks for himself. I didn't even have to kick Albert under the table—he recognized a cue when he heard it. He got up purposefully.

"I must call the *Procureur du Roi*, the Attorney of the King, now. According to our law, he will turn the case over immediately to an Instructing Judge."

He looked directly at Martin. "Most assuredly there is enough evidence to try you for murder and drug dealing. However, Dr. Hirshon, if I knew all the facts and factors of your behavior, it is quite possible that I would tell the *Procureur du Roi* that I suspect you have a 'divergent attitude,' which is our term for abnormal behavior."

Martin sat back. "How would that affect the proceedings?"

"The Instructing Judge would then immediately, within twenty-four hours, have you examined by one or two psychiatrists."

"What would happen if they were convinced

that Martin was psychotic?" I asked. Notice my use of the word "convince," indicating that it would be up to the persuasive performance of the perpetrator to prove to the doctors that he was unable to control his behavior due to aberrational psychosis. Martin's eyes lit up with the thrill of the challenge to prove that he could easily outwit twenty psychiatrists.

"If the Instructing Judge was advised that the perpetrator was indeed not sane, he would not stand trial but would be sent to the Psychiatric Institute at Tournay, an excellent facility where he would be treated until the time when the doctors determined he was totally sane—at which time he would be released."

"What sort of place is this institute?" asked Martin.

"It is the only one in Belgium. I have heard it called 'a very civilized hotel.' "

"And one is confined there for how long?" asked Martin.

"Until the staff physicians ascertain that the patient is cured of his psychosis and is no longer a threat to society."

I could see Martin thinking gleefully, Piece of cake.

"All right," said Martin. "Turn on your tape recorder." He acted like he was about to deliver a lecture at Harvard. Albert read him his rights and asked him if he wanted a lawyer.

"What for? Why should I pay a lawyer? There's nothing going on here that I can't handle," he said arrogantly.

Albert turned on the machine.

"It was really very simple. I wanted to set up an international drug business that would involve a minimum of risk to me. The way to do that is to (a) involve as few partners as possible, (b) give minimal information to underlings and enough financial compensation to keep them happy, plus emotional compensation to keep them loyal. Once I had the plan, all I had to do was find the right people and press the right buttons to get them to join my enterprise."

"What made you choose Iran? It's not one of the renowned international sources for drug trading." It was a point that had been puzzling me.

"Any country where the people are poor and repressed is a receptive environment for drug trading. The stuff is easy to get anywhere—the only problem is distribution."

He described how he had met Mitra and her brother at their father's home and recognized how the repressions imposed upon the youth in Iran could easily be sublimated into political rebellion, which he turned to his advantage by organizing them into the Partisans of God. He created little sorties that made them feel powerful and effective—"a small bomb here and there" was the way he put it.

Setting up the procurement and distribution network was simple. The hardest part was establishing a method of shipping. "When I met Silvia Lopez, I knew I had my source." He smiled and said, "To be charitable, she was not exactly an attractive woman. It was quite easy to get her to do anything I wanted."

I resisted the powerful urge to kick him in the crotch.

"You packed the cocaine in the OSS operational systems software cartons, right?" I asked.

"Right."

"Did Hugh Eddington know about this?"

"Of course. He was the head of SATCOM operations. He had to be involved."

And the Aston Martin and the Saville Row clothing had to be supported.

"So Silvia approved of using her company as a shipping facility for your drug business?" I asked.

"To be quite honest, no," he said.

He had just reaffirmed my distrust of people who use expressions like "to be honest with you" or "to be perfectly frank."

"How did you get her to go along with you?" I asked.

"I used my persuasive charms—she was in love with me, you know—but she had some moral reservations. I've always found that consciences can be swayed by the right appeals, so I gave her the idea of The Naji. She was consumed with her personal transmission project that she saw as a potential boon to mankind. She was furious at those companies who couldn't, as she said, 'share her vision,' " he said contemptuously, "and wouldn't give her the financing."

Incredible. Look who's sneering at insane obsessions.

"I saw how I could use this anger to my advantage. I conceived The Naji plan and told her I would handle the whole thing with my little band of amateur terrorists; no one would get hurt, those tightfisted companies would get justly punished, and she would have her money that would enable her to go ahead with her noble cause. In other words, the end would justify the means.''

He paused and looked around at us with a smile. The son of a bitch was waiting for applause, or at the very least, a "well done."

"All I had to do was alert my group as to when and where specific executives would be in Iran. I do consulting troubleshooting for those companies, so it was easy to get the information. They would accomplish the snatch, following my plan, of course. Those pea-brains wouldn't know how to work their way out of a paper bag without me. Imagine, two of them once had the nerve to ask for a bigger cut of the drug money! They're nothing but mindless mules. It's like the milk wagon horse asking the milkman for a share of his sales.''

I asked him carefully, "Did you give them a bigger share?''

He looked at me in astonishment. "Are you serious? What kind of leader would I be if I allowed my troops to make demands?''

"Weren't they angry when you refused?''

"Of course. I could have explained why I'm entitled to the lion's share, but it's a bad precedent to reason with idiots—so I shot them.''

"How did you explain their deaths to their comrades?''

"That's easy. I told them the Israelis did it and a Spanish attaché had betrayed them to the Israelis.'' He smiled a self-congratulatory smile. "They're just primitive children, you see. They need a focus for their fury and revenge, so I gave one to them. It helps keep up their morale."

I kept checking to be sure the tape recorder was working during this speech, and I shot a look of gratitude to Albert for permitting me to proceed with a line of questioning that had no relevance to his case.

"Who contacted the heads of the companies posing as The Naji?" I asked.

"I did, of course," said Martin. "I'm good at accents, so I put on this posh English accent that for some reason turns middle- and lower-class Brits into servile gullible twits, and that was it. The only time one of my plans didn't work was when you thwarted them, Emma. But that worked out all right for me. It gave me you as a secondary focus to draw their attention away from questioning about the drug money. The Spanish diplomat hunt was wearing thin since no one seemed to be able to locate him."

"You realize they could have killed Emma," said Albert.

Martin shrugged. "Living is a risk. We are born and we die."

Ah, an existentialist—or a Mafia member; the philosophies are the same.

"One thing that puzzles me, Martin. How come you left the one million pounds in Silvia's safe? Surely you had the combination."

He looked at me in surprise. "That was Silvia's money. I had promised it to her in return for her allowing me to use her company for my drug distribution."

I must have looked puzzled by this statement because he became indignant.

"I had given Silvia my word. In business, a man's word is his bond."

I felt like I had stepped through the looking glass. Was I really getting a lecture on business ethics from a murdering, drug-dealing maniac? Albert was also stunned into silence, but he recovered first.

"Ms. Lopez agreed to let you use her company for shipping drugs?" asked Albert.

"Yes." He looked disgustingly self-satisfied. "As I told you, it's really quite easy to get people to do what you want—all it takes is finding their vulnerable spots. Usually, as with Silvia and Hugh, it's sex."

I don't approve of police brutality, but this was one time I thought it might be appropriate.

"Why did you murder her?" asked Albert.

"She suddenly got moral and told me she wouldn't allow her company to be used as my shipping facility anymore. She had heard about today's shipment and wanted to stop it. Imagine— my biggest delivery ever, the one that would take me over the top, and just like a woman, she changes her mind. I couldn't accept that, of course."

"And why Hugh?"

"He figured out that I had killed Silvia. The little slimebucket was willing to go along with drug dealing, but he said he couldn't countenance murder. Imagine the idiocy. He's willing to engage in the sale of drugs that can destroy the lives of thousands of people, but the self-righteous prig lec-

tures to me on the error of the extinction of just one
unimportant woman."

He shook his head as if in wonder about the
strange foibles of Man. Then he continued, telling
his story with such relish that I wondered how law
enforcement officers who listen to horrendous con-
fessions can desist from reacting normally—like
beating the shit out of the confessor. This man's
concepts of morality were incredible.

"If he knew you killed Silvia, wouldn't you think
he might be afraid to meet with you alone in his
flat?" asked Albert.

"Ah, but you're not reckoning with the vanity
and cupidity of the man," Martin said scornfully.
"First, he was exceedingly proud of his superb
physical condition, which he maintained with
faithful daily visits to a health club. He made constant snide references to my lack of fitness—so he
had no doubt that he could defend himself successfully in any physical encounter with me. Secondly, the real reason for the meeting was the
greedy bastard figured that since Silvia was gone,
I needed him more and therefore he wanted a
greater cut. That's when I knew he had to be dis-
posed of."

"Why did you want all that money, Martin?" I
asked. "After all, you live well, you aren't in any
need. What did you plan to do with whatever's in
your Swiss bank account plus this latest huge
coup?"

He looked at me with a cunning smile. "Oh,
didn't I mention my Grand Plan? It's to buy SAT-
COM and become the sole owner of what I will
build into the world's largest software company."

He's speaking in the present tense. The lunatic has an idea that he will accomplish his dream eventually.

"So you had to eliminate both Silvia and Hugh eventually."

He nodded his head. "Ultimately, yes. I didn't plan to do it right now, but when they got in the way of my making the definitive deal that would achieve my financial goal, I had to change my timetable a bit."

"Could you tell us something about your murder methods, Dr. Hirshon?" Albert asked in that dispassionate voice police must assume so as not to let the perpetrator see their revulsion.

"You mean the garrote? Emma was right. I learned how to use it in the Mossad. We need a way of killing quietly and swiftly. Most use a knife, but I've always found the garrote works best for me."

You would have thought he was discussing his preference in golf clubs.

"With Silvia it was easy, of course. My method is to catch people totally unaware. Struggling gets messy. She was brushing her hair and didn't realize what I was doing, until it was too late. Hugh was more difficult. I arranged to meet him at his flat—that's where we always had our little encounters."

He was amused at the look of disgust that Albert tried valiantly but unsuccessfully to hide.

"What's the matter, Commissaire? Does a bit of buggering bother you? I imagine you've done things to men in your work that is far worse. I regard my penis as just another weapon to be used

in the line of duty. Hugh wasn't a full-blown homosexual, if you'll pardon the expression—he
liked women as well as men. Silvia was so starved
for affection that she was easy to convince I adored
her, silly cow. Hugh took a little more persuasion,
but a large dose of flattery and admiration works
wonders on a popinjay like him. Also, we had met
years ago at M.I.T. and I recall Hughie-boy was
known to take his sex either way. He insisted I
meet him at his flat to discuss the 'new developments that will change our business arrangements.'
Not only did he harangue me about the increase in
his financial share, but he then went on and on
about Silvia's missing record of all the drug distribution shipments which he felt was incriminating.
He was distraught because he couldn't find where
she had hidden it."

I was tempted to tell him I had the record and
yes, it was incriminating. Caleb, Albert, and Interpol will undoubtedly check out the names on Silvia's disk just as I had and will easily trace the
shipments back to SATCOM, Hugh, and eventually
Martin. But I hated to interrupt someone when he's
on a roll, nor did I want the police to know I had
seen the disk. I figured I'd have to do another of
my dropped-earring gambits to call it to Caleb's
attention. But actually, Martin was so enchanted
with this opportunity to recount what he perceived
as his brilliant machinations that I doubt an interruption would have staved the flow.

"It took some heavy-duty sex to calm him down,
but I knew he wouldn't hold together long and had
to be eliminated. I anticipated that he'd be tougher
to do than Silvia—I had to stun him first with the

telephone." He smiled craftily. "That's why you couldn't find the weapon, Commissaire. I wiped it off, of course, as well as everything else in the place."

"And where is the garrote, Dr. Hirshon?" Albert asked softly.

"It's right here in my pocket, Commissaire. I always carry it with me. I operate on the 'you never know' principle." And he pulled it out.... "Like *now*."

In seconds, he had the garrote around my neck and everyone froze.

"Now nobody move, or one twist and our sweet Emma will be history."

I didn't like the sound of that, and the damned rope was very tight and uncomfortable. He got up, me with him, of course, and pulled me closely in front of him. At this point in time, wherever he goest, I goest.

"Now I want everyone to sit exactly where you are. I'm taking us out of here."

"Where will you go, Doctor?" Albert asked calmly.

"Oh, I'm not going to do something as stupid as asking for a car and a helicopter. Emma and I are just going to melt into the thousands of people milling around this busy airport and walk right out of here. You can't risk discharging firearms at us with all those innocent men, women, and children dashing about. And if any one of you gets close, remember all it takes is one strong twist and it's farewell Emma."

Unfortunately, I couldn't use my greatest weapon to dissuade him of his course of action—

my voice didn't work because of the garrote. But I did have my second best weapon. I reached around behind me and squeezed his balls with all my might. I can still hear his scream in my ears—he doubled over in agony. I have pretty strong hands thanks to my working out with weights, and my strong instinct for survival made them even stronger.

Albert was pale with relief as they took Martin away.

"My God, Emma, he could've killed you," he said, his voice breaking. "I was so frightened."

You? Me!

I hated to do it, but we had to play parts of the tape for Mitra. As she heard Martin telling how he had killed her brother and cousin, and duped her and her associates, tears started streaming down her cheeks and her whole body sagged in the wheelchair. It was almost cruel, but necessary for her to communicate the truth to her group so that the vendetta against Bernardo would be lifted. It is always painful to have to face the fact that you've been wrong and done foolish things, but at twenty it's even harder. She phoned her father because she would need legal help. It was pathetic: the defiance was gone and all that remained was a frightened little girl.

Two hours later, we all sat around in Albert's office—me, Albert, and Luis. I had called Abba and Caleb and they were both flying in.

"Are you going to advise the *Procureur du Roi* that Martin is of 'divergent attitude'?" I asked.

"No," said Albert.

"Why am I not surprised?" I said.

"I think," he said with careful deliberation, "that Martin Hirshon is an evil human being who knew exactly what he was doing. He's not insane, just an obnoxious egotist filled with an overblown sense of entitlement that causes him to view all other mortals as lesser than he and therefore expendable."

"That young woman in the wheelchair—how much in drugs was she carrying?" asked Luis.

"Eight kilos of cocaine . . . incredible how much one leg can hold," Albert said with obvious satisfaction. "That was a good idea checking out her own wheelchair when it came through baggage, Emma. Three kilos in the padding. How did you know?" he asked me.

"First I want to know what he is doing here," I said, pointing my head toward Luis.

"Don Luis is our informant," said Albert. "He graciously offered to be here in case we needed an Iranian interpreter."

"That call you got in Bruges," I said to Luis. "And Silvia, too."

"Yes. My source in the Partisans of God told me. I, of course, notified Inspector Heist."

"I have another question, Luis. Why did you lie to us and say you had just arrived in Wycombe on Friday when you had actually arrived the day before?"

He looked dumbfounded.

"I saw the date on your train ticket."

His face cleared, then started to turn pink. "Yes, I did come to High Wycombe a day earlier than I said. I—er—had some special business to take care of."

I looked at him and suddenly comprehension dawned. "It's the beauteous Miss Ballard, isn't it?"

He shifted uncomfortably in his chair.

"Come on, Luis, there's nothing wrong with having it on with your secretary. She seems like a lovely woman."

I just knew Tyrone Power couldn't be the bad guy.

Then Albert asked, "How did you know this Martin Hirshon? Who is he?"

I told them the whole story while trying to play down Abba's involvement, because I know how law enforcement departments hate to have their territories impinged upon by foreign law agencies. Suddenly a thought hit me.

"My God, poor Esther. She adores the man. She'll be shattered. Who's going to tell her?"

XXI

"ESTHER IS A soldier, Emma. She took it like a soldier," said Abba as he sat with me, Albert, Caleb, and Luis on my balcony at Avenue Hamoir overlooking the park. It was four in the afternoon, and Abba and Caleb had just flown in for a confab celebration.

"Besides, she had an inkling when she saw the garrote marks on Hugh Eddington. She knew that was Martin's specialty in the Mossad . . . it virtually became his trademark."

I suddenly remembered my surprise at Esther's strong reaction when we found Hugh. Since killing and bodies were fairly commonplace to her, I recalled a sense of something being not quite appropriate.

The Israeli looked like a big teddy bear as he sat back sipping his drink.

"The poor kid has to know that the bastard was using her and the marriage was based on shit. He told us calmly that he married her to get a job with her father. It fit perfectly into his plan, which was apparently to be the biggest cocaine distributor in Europe. The job required him to be based in Brussels and travel all over the Continent selling Israeli engineering services—a perfect cover."

"Esther told me he was a brilliant engineer."

Abba shook his head. "That's the sad thing. About eight years ago, he developed a special engine and tried to get backing to produce it. He raised some money but not enough, and foolishly went ahead, like so many novices with a dream who think all you need is a great idea. The old saying that if you build a better mousetrap the world will beat a path to your door is bullshit. Today if you don't have big bucks to market the mousetrap to the world, all you'll end up with is the cheese. He thought he'd become a millionaire; instead, like hundreds of other small underfinanced start-up companies, he went bust. So with his ego, not to mention his pocketbook, shattered by failure, I guess his imperative was to tell the world, 'Fuck you, I'll get mine'—and there's no faster way to do that than pushing drugs."

"Abba, your psych degree from Brooklyn College is showing."

"I think," said Albert, "that in Abba's business, as well as mine and that of the chief superintendent here, a knowledge of human reaction and interaction is vital."

"For the criminal as well," I said. "Look at how Martin Hirshon used psychology to get the Partisans of God to work for him."

"He played it shrewd there, all right," said Abba. "He tells them he's a renegade Jew who now believes in their cause—everyone loves a repenting sinner—and he's got a great way to raise money for weapons. They go for it, and he has a small army of working mules at bargain prices. He tells them they're getting fifty percent of the take—but their cut is no more than twenty percent. When two of the schmucks become suspicious, he kills them. Beautiful."

"Turning those murders to his advantage by blaming it on Bernardo—one must admit he's adroit," said Luis.

"The guy's a bloody genius. The Partisans were losing their enthusiasm for the cause—with their I.Q.'s, they probably have an attention span of four seconds. They were getting slow and sloppy, and he felt the *putzim* needed a shot in the ass to get them up again. After he blew those guys away, he figured he'd use the killing to give the boys and girls a raison d'etre—so he blames it on the Israelis. The best way to inflame the infidels is always to say the Jews did it. Listen, throughout history we've been blamed for everything but the fall of Pompeii and the Chicago fire—it's a wonder they didn't say it was Mrs. Ginsberg's cow instead of Mrs. O'Leary's."

"And Bernardo happened to have been in Israel just before the killing so I guess he was the perfect patsy," I said.

"Speaking of perfect patsies, I feel like a major asshole," said Abba. "I come on like the big hero to save you from the bad guys and I send you right into the home of the head bad guy."

I walked over and put my arm around his big burly shoulders. "It's nice to know that the famous

Mossad is human and makes mistakes."

"Who said anything about the Mossad?" he said in mock seriousness. "You know that's a secret organization."

"You mean you guys stopped wearing those T-shirts?"

Caleb lifted his glass of cider and said, "Gentlemen, a toast to Ms. Emma Rhodes—Jane Marple, Jessica Fletcher, and Ava Gardner all rolled up into one. She cleared up our cases and made us all look like heroes. I think, as you Americans say, Emma, we owe you one."

I acknowledged their toast by nodding graciously and then turned to Caleb. "Ava Gardner?"

He grinned. "I've seen *Mogambo* six times."

"Maybe he thought she was Erle Stanley's sister," said Abba. He put his arm around me and said like a proud parent, "*Al'hakefach*, I feel good because my sharp shiksa here has a large payoff in her future—and she resolved her case in nine days without getting killed or even hurt."

"Thanks in no small measure to you and your Jewish Boy Scout troop," I added.

Caleb looked puzzled. "What's all this about?" he asked.

Abba looked at me in surprise. "You mean you haven't told the chief superintendent the real identity of Emma Rhodes, Private Resolver?"

Caleb looked thunderstruck. "You're a private detective?" he asked incredulously.

"Not exactly," I answered. "It's sort of complicated. Why don't we leave it for later and I'll explain all over dinner tonight. Now how about we have another drink and some more nibbles?"

Abba refilled his plate. "Pretty nice spread you rustled up on short notice, pardner," he said. "Here I thought you were just a toothsome babe, a *chatichah* with a brain. I figured your kitchen expertise was strictly confined to opening take-out containers. You know, I might seriously think of marrying you, but somehow I can't envision you lighting candles every Friday night."

I saw the pained look on Albert's face when Abba mentioned marriage. I had told him conclusively that I would not marry him. It takes a while for a man's ego to absorb the blow of a turned-down proposal, and a little longer to get over the broken heart. I should know, I've rejected twenty-two to date. Hey, remember I'm thirty-five and my first proposal was from the star fullback of the Rye High football team when I was all of seventeen. As I vaguely remember, he had the body of a god and the brain of an escargot.

I couldn't really blame Albert for being unhappy when he looked at me. Usually when I meet with a recent rejectee I try to look as untempting as possible. I'm not a mean person, you see, just a highly selective one. But this time there were two other men present and I had another audience to consider. I was wearing the charcoal gray wool crepe trousers I had made in Rome last year that I call my diet control pants; they're sized to allow room for a thumb to slip in before a meal and the pinky after. My motto is "pants tight, eat light" . . . words to live by. My top was a fitted black cotton sweater and jewelry was the Elsa Peretti Silver Flask on a chain. The outfit is simple but guaranteed to evoke a silent or audible whistle, depending on the neighborhood.

"I'm glad you're enjoying the hors d'oeuvres, Abba," I said as I eyed his loaded plate. I wasn't worried because there were ample refills in the kitchen. It was my "instant cocktail party" creation: caviared cream cheese, anchovies and pimentos, and for the hot dish, kielbasa rounds in hot currant sauce. It involves one short trip to the store, if I don't happen to have all the ingredients in my cupboard, which I always do, but this isn't my home. In my lifestyle, dropping in for drinks is a frequent social occurrence so I am always prepared. The caviar (not Beluga, of course—usually white fish roe that is called caviar) is piled and smoothed over a mound of whipped cream cheese. The hot currant sauce is ketchup, vinegar, and currant jelly (any jam or honey will do) that are boiled together for a minute; Worcestershire sauce and Tabasco can be added at whim. The anchovies and pimentos are mixed together and chives sprinkled on top. Now these goodies may sound like they owe more to Martha Stewart than Julia Child, but they look impressive, taste good, and go great with booze, so who really cares if they get the Good Housekeeping rather than Cordon Bleu seal of approval?

"Yes, we are all heroes and heroines," said Albert as we all settled down on the balcony again. "But my heart suffers for Dona Isabella and Don Roderigo, who lost a daughter, and Luis here, who lost a sister."

Luis bowed his head in thanks.

"And my anguish," I said sadly, "is for poor Silvia, who lost her self-respect and life in that one moment when she saw Martin approach her with a garrote and realized that their loving relationship was a sham."

"That *kus amack* motherfucking scumbag," Abba said angrily. "And he had to be a Jew."

I noted Albert's discomfort at Abba's language in front of a lady (that's me). Caleb hadn't lifted an eyebrow. They were both the same age and in the same profession, but while the lawmen I know have developed a jaundiced eye toward all mankind and womankind, Albert has managed to separate his work world from his social one and treats his female friends with a gentlemanly protectiveness. Although his old-world attitude was charming to visit, I'd find it hell to live with.

Caleb looked sympathetically at Abba's furious face and said softly, " 'Hath not a Jew eyes? Hath not a Jew hands, organs, dimensions, senses, affections, passions? If you prick us, do we not bleed? If you tickle us, do we not laugh? If you poison us, do we not die?' Abba, if Shakespeare accepted the right of a Jew to be an ordinary feeling human being, why can't you? And part of being human is to err."

"Shakespeare and Alexander Pope in one statement, most impressive, Detective Superintendent," I said admiringly. "But the really chilling aspect is that Martin doesn't see that he erred. Silvia refused to allow him to continue distributing cocaine through her company because she felt it was wrong. But the only wrong Martin could comprehend was to himself."

"That Naji plan was pretty damned sharp," said Caleb.

Abba nodded his head in agreement. "The guy's a prick, but a brilliant prick," he said.

"It's sort of an everyone-wins situation," said Caleb. "The CEO who pays The Naji and gets his man back looks like a hero to his board of directors because he saved them thousands of pounds and enhanced their corporate image, and Silvia gets her money to build her product."

"Yes," I said, "but what about those poor kidnapped guys who lived in horrible conditions and in fear of their lives for days?"

"Ach," Abba said with a wave of his hand. "I've seen Outward Bound camps that put you through worse. Besides, the experience probably did them good."

I was incredulous. "Abba, chicken soup does you good. I've heard of all sorts of bizarre cures for ills, but shivering in the cold awaiting imminent death was never one of them, not even in California."

"I'm not talking body health, I'm talking emotional health. I'll bet every one of those guys came back with a different and better set of values. Expecting to die does that for you. You get a sudden epiphany on what a shitty life you've been leading and you vow to change. I betcha they spend more time with their families now."

"I grant you the experience may have had a salubrious effect on them," said Caleb, "but the therapy is a bit drastic, don't you think, Abba?"

I was silent for a moment. "Gentlemen, if you all owe me one, I'm calling in my chit now."

They looked at me. Abba groaned. "I knew there had to be a catch."

"I'd like you all to omit the Naji scam from your reports."

"What?"

"Why?"

"Are you nuts?"

"Look, you have Martin Hirshon on enough counts. What crime did he actually commit as The Naji?"

"For starters, extortion," said Caleb. "Then there's kidnapping."

"I'm not defending him, for sure, but he didn't do the kidnapping, the Partisans did. He promised to return the victims, and he did."

"Why do you want these episodes quashed, Emma?" asked Albert.

"Because they smear Silvia and dishonor her memory and to what end? She died a heroine in the cause of preventing dissemination of drugs. For her sake and that of her family, why can't we just leave it at that?"

Luis came over, his eyes filled with tears, and bent over to kiss my hand. Abba, Caleb, and Albert looked at each other and nodded.

"Deal?" I asked.

"Deal!" they all agreed.

"Caleb, why don't you give the story to that young eager reporter from the *High Wycombe Times* who was bugging us? It'll be the making of his career and he'll take the facts as you give them. Instead of everyone licking their prurience-loving chops over 'Heiress Murdered in Love Nest,' they can be reading the story of an admirable young woman who lost her life because she had a conscience."

I suddenly looked at my watch and jumped up. "Guys, I have to get going. I'm meeting a plane from Switzerland and I have to pick up Felippa first. Make yourselves at home," I said, looking at Abba and Caleb. "I'll see you when I get back tonight."

Albert looked puzzled. "You mean they are staying here—overnight?"

"Yes, Albert," I said.

"Don't worry, Inspector," Caleb said with a half smile. "There's safety in numbers."

"Not where I grew up," said Abba.

"Abba, behave yourself," I said, laughing.

"If I behaved myself, *tsotskele*, we would have never met."

"How did you two unlikely mates meet anyway?" asked Caleb. "I have a feeling there's quite a story to it."

"You're fuckin'-A right on the mark, Caleb. It was I don't remember how many years ago," said Abba. "I was a soldier then in Hebron guarding the Temple Mosque that's constant *tsuras* because it's sacred to both Jews and Moslems since it's Abraham's tomb. You get Moslems praying to Abraham, the father of Ishmael and his descendents, and Jews praying to Abraham, father of Isaac and his descendents. These are two groups that don't go well together, so you can imagine when they have to share a sacred shrine. Anyway, I was on an off duty break, sitting and eating an apple, when this young juicy Arab girl approaches and comes on to me big time. Well, I'm a healthy young male so I respond. All of a sudden she starts to rip her clothes . . ."

I picked it up from there. "I was visiting the tomb with my Polaroid camera and suddenly I notice this girl ripping her clothes. Being a total ignoramus about theology, I immediately figure this is some sort of weird religious ritual that I'm lucky to see, so I start photographing. Then she starts to scream in some unintelligible language, and I see from the reaction of the Arab males who come to her rescue that what she's hollering is, 'RAPE.' "

"The Arabs are ready to castrate me on the spot," continued Abba. "The Israeli MPs are trying to pull them off me. And into the middle of this howling mess walks this glamorous creature yelling and waving a picture. She finally gets the attention of one of the MPs, and the eyes of all the Arab males—shall I tell them how, Emma?"

"Well, I saw that drastic measures were required," I said, "or this poor innocent Israeli soldier would shortly lose the important testimonials to his circumcision. So I started to remove my blouse."

Albert and Luis gasped. Caleb roared.

"It worked like a charm," said Abba. "All action stopped—and she was able to show them the pictures proving the girl herself had torn her clothes and not me in some wild moment of rapacious passion—not that I've never done that but only in the case of consulting adults." He looked over at me fondly. "We've been friends ever since."

Albert was still shaken by the recitation. "Whatever made you react so—er, strongly, Emma?" he asked.

"Because I despise women who fake rape for their own sleazy reasons and make it difficult for actually raped women to be believed."

I got up to leave. "So long, gentlemen. I'll be back for dinner." I turned to Abba. "Don't tire yourself over a hot stove tonight, dearie. Why don't we all go out?"

I had told Felippa that a man was coming in from Switzerland who might know something about Bernardo's whereabouts and I needed her to answer some questions that might come up. As we drove to the airport, she was nervous and her eyes showed evidence of the weeks of worry and tension.

We stood at the gate. The first man off the plane was a tall, handsome man in a well-cut gray sports jacket and black turtleneck whose face looked bone-weary but whose posture was regally erect.

"Bernardo!" Felippa ran forward and threw her arms around him. The other passengers smiled as they passed the couple, who were locked in an embrace. When they released each other, I saw tears were streaming down both their cheeks.

"*Gracias*, darling Emma," said Felippa, and she reached out to kiss my hand. She looked up at her husband with love pouring from her eyes, and then turned to me. "I had been *sin vida, sin esperanza*— now you have given me life. How did you find him, how did you do this . . . ?"

"I knew that Luis must be hiding him in one of his houses. It wouldn't be the one in Morocco because there are too many ties to Islam extremists there. So obviously, it had to be the ski house in Switzerland. I just waited for the all clear to sound before sending for him. Now, why don't you two go home to Juanito. We'll talk tomorrow. I know the queen will want to hear the whole story."

The next day when I entered Fabiola's sitting room in the palace, I was startled to see so many people there. Fabiola, Felippa, and Bernardo with little Juan, Luis, and Dona Isabella and Don Roderigo. The queen smiled as she patted the place on the couch next to her, inviting me to sit. She looked regal in a pink silk jacket dress with two strands of the loveliest pearls I have ever seen and matching earrings.

"We are all family here, my dear Emma. We wish to know the details of what you did for us. Please, tell us."

They listened intently as I related the entire story, omitting nothing. When I came to the parts about the attempts on my life, the room resounded in gasps and "*Madre Dios!*"

"I never realized that what you were doing for us could put your life in jeopardy," Felippa said emphatically. "I would never have forgiven myself if anything had happened to you."

As for the details about Silvia's activities and death, I looked over at her parents and hesitated. But Don Roderigo shook his head and said, "No. Do not try to spare us, please. This is our family here, they must know everything."

I looked appealingly at Luis—how much is everything? Luis nodded and said softly, "I have told them. In our family, we do not flinch from the truth."

A noble sentiment—but sometimes cruel.

I saw tears on the cheeks of the queen and Fe-

lippa as I described the details of Silvia's murder.
When I had completed my narration, the room was
silent. Then Bernardo walked over and stood directly in front of me.

"Señorita Emma, you have saved my family and
my honor. To us that is more than life itself. I owe
you a debt that time can never erase and money
cannot repay. You know that you have our eternal
gratitude."

I'm a sucker for eloquence, but I really would
rather have the cash.

He stood there, just looking at me, then he held
out his hand. For one terrible moment, I thought
he was just going to shake my hand. He did, but
to my relief, there was an envelope in it. Felippa
came over and kissed me on both cheeks. "We are
going home to Madrid today. Please remember,
Emma, that *mi casa es su casa* always."

After they left, two footmen entered wheeling
trays of wine and tapas, the marvelous Spanish
food appetizers the Spanish serve with drinks. I
hadn't had too many of my own hors d'oeuvres,
so I pigged out on hot empanadas, *pastelitos frituras
de carne*, and *bolitas de camarónes*. Like the waiters
in restaurants who always seem to come over to
ask "how's everything?" just when you can't answer, Luis caught me with a mouthful.

"Emma, my parents and I are very grateful for
what you have done for Silvia and her memory."

"Now that Hugh and Silvia are gone, who's
minding the store, Luis?" I asked.

"You are looking at the new president of SAT-
COM LTD.," said Don Roderigo, who had just
joined us. He looked at Luis proudly and then his

eyes clouded. "Sometimes good can come from evil."

"I'm sure he'll do a marvelous job," I said.

Luis took my hand and held it. "It is you who has done the truly marvelous job." He looked deeply into my eyes. "Thank you."

Miss Ballard, I almost envy you. However, as I said before, he may be a gorgeous Tyrone Power look-alike, but he just doesn't make my juices flow.

When it was time to leave, Fabiola came over to me.

"You know that what Bernardo said applies to me as well. We Spanish consider that a debt of honor is assumed by the entire family." She then kissed me on both cheeks. "To echo Felippa, *mi casa es su casa* always."

I was at the door, ready to walk out, when Dona Isabella handed me a package. "I want you to have this," she said softly.

Of course, I didn't open the envelope or the package in the palace. I was taught that the gracious way to receive a gift is to thank the giver profusely without looking at it, thus indicating that it's not the gift itself but the idea of giving for which you are grateful. This behavior not only attests to your excellent manners and fine upbringing, but also saves you from the difficulty of summoning up sincere thanks when you unwrap the package and find a ruffled pink gingham toilet paper cover. When I got inside my apartment, I dropped my bag on the table and ripped open the envelope. 608,000 Belgian francs. That's about $20,000 for a little over ten days' work. Is this a great business or what? Eat your heart out, Kinsey

Milhone, V. I. Warshawski, and Jim Rockford. I hollered for Abba and Caleb, but they had probably gone out for a walk. I took Dona Isabella's package into the living room and flipped on the TV as I passed. I ripped off the paper and dropped to the couch, staring at what I held in my hand. It was the small Picasso sketch.